A Day at the Inn, A Night at the Palace
and Other Stories

Also by Catherine Lundoff

Crave: Tales of Lust, Love and Longing
Night's Kiss: Lesbian Erotica

as editor
Haunted Hearths and Sapphic Shades:
Lesbian Ghost Stories

editor with JoSelle Vanderhooft
Hellebore and Rue: Tales of Queer Women and Magic

A Day at the Inn, A Night at the Palace

and Other Stories

Catherine Lundoff

Lethe Press
Maple Shade, NJ

These stories are fiction.

Published by Lethe Press, 118 Heritage Ave, Maple Shade, NJ 08052.
lethepressbooks.com   lethepress@aol.com
Book design: Toby Johnson

ISBN-10: 1-59021-378-5
ISB-13: 978-1-59021-378-0

Library of Congress Cataloging-in-Publication data
available upon request.

Credits

The Egyptian Cat" reprinted from *Tales of the Unanticipated.* Vol. 30, 2010, Eric Heideman, ed. / "The Letter of Marque" reprinted from *Lacuna: A Journal of Historical Fiction*. October 2010, Megan Arkenberg, ed. / "Great Reckonings, Little Rooms" reprinted from *Time Well Bent: Queer Alternate History*. Lethe Press, 2009. Connie Wilkins, ed. / "Regency Masquerade" reprinted from *Kissed By Venus*, May 2008. Alexandra Wolfe, ed. Originally published in the *Harrington Lesbian Fiction Quarterly*. Vol. 3 (1), Alice Street Editions, 2002. / "Vadija" reprinted from *Such a Pretty Face: Tales of Power and Abundance*. Meisha Merlin, 2000. Lee Martindale, ed. / "A Scent of Roses" reprinted from *So Fey: Queer Fairy Fiction*. Lethe Press, 2009. Steve Berman, ed. / "M. Le Maupin" reprinted from *Lesbian Short Fiction,* Vol. 3, 1997. Jinx Beers, ed. / "Spell, Book and Candle" reprinted from *Khimairal Ink*, January 2008. Carrie Tierney, ed. / "Red Scare" reprinted from *Simulacrum*, Vol. 1 (2). January 2004. Lynne Jamneck, ed. / "A Day at the Inn, A Night at the Palace" is original to this volume.

Table of Contents

For Jana, once again, and for all the editors and readers who have encouraged me to write over the years. With many additional thanks to Steve Berman of Lethe Press who always asks for more.

Introduction

I first began writing fiction in 1996 during my ill-fated foray into law school at the University of Iowa. I had just closed my bookstore and was looking for something to occupy me for the next couple of years while my partner, now wife, completed her papermaking apprenticeship. Law school didn't just make me miserable, it made me telekinetic. I broke plates with my mind simply by walking into the room. I know it sounds far-fetched, but it's all true.

In a desperate effort to preserve sanity and what was left of the kitchen, Jana suggested that I try writing a book. I was so excited by the prospect that I not only started writing a nonfiction book, I wrote my first short story at the same time. That story was "M. Le Maupin," which you will find collected here, though slightly changed from the original. I submitted it to a little magazine called *Lesbian Short Fiction* and much to my surprise, it was accepted. And artist Alicia Austin drew an amazing cover for the magazine based on my story. I was hooked. I was going to be a writer. Law school vanished into the distance.

Fast forward to the current era and I've written a lot of short fiction since that first story. In addition to my lesbian erotica, which is collected elsewhere, there were romances, historical swashbuckling adventures, fantasies, science fiction, alternate histories and sundry other tales about queer women and men.

I grew up reading Dumas and Sabatini and Hope, dreaming about more active roles for their women characters. As I got older I researched the lives of real women who were pirates or who took up the sword and had adventures so it's not too surprising that I would write about those women when I first put cursor to screen. Some of the fruits of that research are collected here. Aubigny Le Maupin and pirate Jacquotte Delahaye were real women, and some of the events in "Great Reckonings, Little Rooms" did occur the way I wrote about them.

Other events and other stories are more speculative. Considerably more speculative: other worlds, things that might have been, magic, all of these have always been a source of fascination and inspiration for me. My stories explore love magic gone wrong, a planet settled by humans who use noir films as the basis for their culture, the authorship of Shakespeare's plays and the death of Christopher Marlowe as well as the perils of editing for small horror presses, among other things.

But I think I've said enough. It's been a wild ride getting here and I hope you enjoy the fruits of that journey.

Catherine Lundoff
Summer 2011

The Egyptian Cat

Erica turned over the last page of the manuscript with a sigh. Somehow, a collection like *Hairballs Over Innsmouth* should have been more fun to edit. She wondered why writers were having such a hard time writing humorous cat-related horror stories that included an homage to H. P. Lovecraft. It should have been a snap. But perhaps the rewrites would look much better.

The thought cheered her enough to go and get the mail, even though it might contain yet more manuscripts. And it did. But along with the envelopes with addresses written in crayon and the one that seemed to contain nothing but melted chocolate, there was a box. She looked at it carefully, noting that although her name and address were printed on a mailing label, the return address was completely illegible.

She wondered if she should contact the bomb squad or something before she opened it. You couldn't be too careful these days. Some of the writers who she'd turned down for her last anthology, *Catnip and Hashish*, had been pretty irate.

Finally she decided she was overreacting. Her writers were cat people, after all; their limited attention span would have moved on to some new source of fascination or irritation by now. She swept up all the mail and dumped it on the dining room table.

She opened the bills first, of course, then the manuscripts, but her gaze was drawn repeatedly back to the mysterious box. Something about it spoke of unfathomable mysteries beyond human ken.

So, after she had opened everything else, separated the mail into piles and fed the cats when their cries became too inconvenient to ignore, she reached for it. First she held it up to her ear to listen for telltale ticking sounds. The brown paper crackled reassuringly but apart from that, the package made no other sound. She cut open a flap in the paper on one side. Nothing leaped out or blew up.

She slowly removed the paper to reveal a completely nondescript cardboard box. Maybe it was shoes. Would a fan have sent her something as useful as a new pair of shoes? She doubted it. One of the cats uttered a piercing whine and she jumped. The cat, a large tabby named Sarnath, rubbed himself ingratiatingly against her leg while she pondered the box. *Open it*, the cat seemed to be saying. *It might be treats*.

"It might be a bad thing too, Sarny. You just never know." She reflected that living alone had left her with the unfortunate habit of talking to her cats. And listening to them. Sarnath's inscrutable slitted gaze met hers and she reached for the box as if under a spell. She opened it, though not without a remaining qualm or two.

But if she had hoped to see its contents immediately, she was doomed to disappointment. Whatever it was, it was buried under styrofoam peanuts that crinkled and rolled beneath her questing fingers.

But at last they encountered something hard. She shivered, then forced herself to grasp whatever it was and pull it from its nest. For a brief instant, she looked away only to find herself looking deep into Sarnath's eyes. The cat had begun to purr, a deep, rumbling noise that should have been reassuring but somehow only served to fill her with a vague apprehension.

With an effort, she turned her head to look at the contents of the package, now cradled gingerly in her right hand. Slitted emerald eyes stared back at her and she very nearly dropped whatever it was. Regaining control, she found her jaw falling open in astonishment. Her unknown admirer had sent her a statue of a cat. And what a statue it was!

Clearly of Egyptian origin, it was made of some sort of black stone and covered with carvings that appeared to be hieroglyphs. A single gold earring hung from one ear and the eyes were greenest glass. Or were they tiny emeralds? She couldn't be sure. She set it down so that it met her gaze with an impassive expression, filling her with both a nameless dread and an unexpected excitement, as if her life could be completely transformed at any moment.

It was at that same moment the doorbell rang, causing Erica to start from her reverie. Surely it couldn't be Mr. McGillicuddy from next door again. He'd already dropped by three times this week and one could only borrow so many cups of sugar. Perhaps Phyllis and Felicia from her bridge club were right and he was interested in more than the contents of her kitchen. She groaned. If only…but there was no point in dwelling on what might have been.

The doorbell rang again, impatience clear in the length of the chime that echoed through the hall. Erica resigned herself to answering it. "Coming! Give me a minute." She remembered to look through the gauzy curtain that hung over the door before she opened it. Even in Foggy Harbor, Massachusetts, there were criminals inclined to prey on a woman living alone.

But all she could see was that the person on her doorstep was broad of shoulder and wearing an elegant suit and a hat that covered her/his hair. He or she also had their back to the door and was looking out over the garden. She did catch a glimpse of dark golden brown skin as the person, whoever they were, raised one hand to brush away some speck on the beautiful dark gray suit. Erica's pulse raced and she tried in vain to catch her breath. *It couldn't be...*

She admonished herself to stop acting like a schoolgirl. Rashida Simmons was gone for good, along with any hopes she'd had in that quarter. Still she trembled as she reached for the knob and opened the door.

Her visitor turned, almost reluctantly, as if they too feared what they might see. An involuntary cry escaped Erica's lips. The woman on her doorstep pulled off her hat and ran her fingers through her short curls. She didn't look up from the threshold as she spoke, "Hello, Erica. I'm sorry for dropping by like this. I'd have called if...I had the number."

At that moment, Erica forgot the ten years that stretched between them, forgot the professional editor that she'd become and spoke her mind without hesitation or forethought. "Rashida Simmons, you get your ass in here right now! You've got some explaining to do!" She reached out with the strength born of desperation and yanked the other woman's arm, pulling her inside. With shaking hands she locked the door behind her, sealing off any chance of easy escape.

Only then did she turn, chest heaving with pent-up indignation. Her quarry met her eyes this time as she took a deep breath and murmured, "It wasn't like that, Erica. I had to leave Foggy Harbor. Let me try and explain but before I go any further, I have to ask: did you receive a package in the mail today?"

"You just drop by after no word for ten years to inquire about the local postal service? Things a little slow wherever you've been keeping yourself?" Erica shook in every limb, part of her longing to hurl herself into Rashida's arms, part of her wanting to throw her out, never to be seen again.

Rashida winced but persisted. "Did it?"

"Yes. Why? Was it from you? Not that a token of affection wouldn't have been too much to ask." Erica uttered a most unladylike snort.

"Where is it?" Rashida ignored the snort, spinning around on her heels as if the statue would be lying around the foyer. She strode around purposefully, looking into each room as if she were welcome to do so. Erica sputtered indignantly after her as she discovered the study. "At last!" she cried out as she dropped into the chair in front of the statue.

The words were a spear through Erica's heart. She forced that organ to harden around a rapidly widening hole. "Well, now that you've found what you came for, I suggest you take it and get out."

Rashida studied her with large golden eyes, almost amber in the afternoon light. Erica strangled stillborn the memory of what they looked like at dawn when her former lover first awakened. She tapped her foot impatiently, waiting for Rashida to take her statue and go.

Instead, the other woman leaned her arms on the table and gave her a serious look. "I know you better than that, Erica. You could never have changed this much. Besides, you're editing cat horror anthologies. You have to know why I'm here; you'll never be able to sleep until you find out."

So Rashida had been following her career? The idea was somehow soothing, warming the coldness of the hard-edged hole in the center of Erica's being. Perhaps…but no. She forced the hope away. Still, it would be nice to know what all this was about. Rashida was right about that much.

She propelled her response out between frozen lips: "Oh, very well. But you'll leave after you're done explaining. I suppose you want tea?" Not gracious certainly, but far more than she intended. She cursed the good manners she'd been brought up with.

"Tea would be wonderful. Thank you." Rashida smiled, and it was like watching dawn over the harbor. Erica very nearly melted, only just forcing herself to flee the room in search of cups and hot water. Rashida trailed after her into the kitchen, giving her no time to recover.

"You've done a lot with the place since your aunt died. I like it." She held the words out like a peace offering and Erica grimaced, knowing that the ceiling was covered with cracked and peeling paint and the random stains of old leaks. Her small inheritance and the income from her books were scarcely enough to pay the property taxes and her own needs, certainly not enough for upkeep in a place this big.

A quiet rage filled her. "I'm engaged. To be married. To Mr. McGillicuddy next door." She blurted the words out, unable to stop herself.

Rashida's dark face paled and she looked away, as if from something she could not bear to see. At last, she murmured, "Congratulations," so softly that Erica barely caught the word.

She cursed the impulse that made her invent such a patent falsehood and longed to throw herself at Rashida's feet to beg for forgiveness. But pride held her upright, made her pour the tea and seal her lips.

Rashida rose, pacing, as she blew on her tea to cool it, her agitation clear. "I had hoped…well, never mind about that now. Can we go back to the other room? I hate to let the statue out of my sight for long." She walked out the door and down the hall without a backward glance or even the saucer that Erica held out to her.

Erica followed her down the hallway, already making up her mind to admit that she'd told a little fib about Mr. McGillicuddy. But when she got to the study, Rashida was sitting at the table, eyes fixed on the cat, and she found she couldn't say it. Instead, she picked up Rashida's cup and smacked it onto the saucer with unnecessary force. "All right, so it's clear that you didn't come back to see me. What's the story about the statue?"

Rashida brought both hands up to her face and rubbed her cheeks as if suddenly exhausted. "All right. You remember when my mother disappeared?"

As if Erica could forget the most traumatic moment of their high school years. Mrs. Simmons had vanished into the night, leaving only the briefest of notes for her husband and teenage daughter. She had assured them that she'd be back and told them not to worry. They never heard from her again.

Erica had spent months consoling Rashida; it had been what had drawn them together. How ironic that Mrs. Simmons' disappearance was somehow instrumental in today's events, too. "Of course I remember. The FBI never found a thing. Your father became a private detective but he never found any trace of her. Why? Have you heard something?"

Rashida reached into the front pocket of her immaculately tailored suit and pulled out a crumpled envelope. Wordlessly, she handed it to Erica. For an instant, Erica contemplated refusing to read whatever it was. After all, what did it matter now? But her curiosity was aroused. She took it, opening the envelope slowly and carefully as if something inside might bite her. A distant part of her brain noted the two-year-old postmark.

The letter inside was typed on an actual typewriter; there were even smudges where the correction tape failed.

My dearest daughter,

I hope you can forgive me. There's no time to try to explain it all now - it wouldn't be good enough for what you've lost anyway. Just know I always meant to come back and that I love you and your father very much. If I hadn't left, I'd have lost both of you.

Now I have to ask you to do something for me. My family, generation upon generation back to our ancestors' time in Nubia of old, were appointed as the guardians of a sacred relic. It is an object of great power and it must be protected from those who would misuse it. The time has come when I must pass it onto you, my child. I know you have started your training and are almost ready to take on this great burden. I will come to you soon to tell you more.

If you do not hear from me again, know that I am prevented from coming by forces beyond my control. I will send the object into safekeeping with friends who will guard it until you are ready.

Return to the beginning to seek what you need.

Your loving mother,
Keira

"I never heard from her again. I believe that she may have run afoul of forces trying to find the statue. I think my aunt and uncle knew what befell her, but feared to tell me in case her fate frightened me from performing my duties," Rashida offered up in spectral tones.

"Not to be overly skeptical, Rashida, but are you sure that your mother was quite...right when she wrote this? Or that this letter is even from her? What 'training'? What sacred relic?" Erica's questions all rushed together until they emerged almost as a single sentence. She bit back a few others. *Nubia? The Simmons family has been here in Foggy Harbor for generations.*

"Still the same old cautious Erica." Rashida smiled wistfully as she took the letter from Erica's hand and carefully folded it before putting it in the envelope and tucking it back in her suit. "My aunt and uncle came to visit about a week before I left Foggy Harbor. They told me some of this back then but I didn't believe it either. Not at first. But then they showed me some things and I...had to leave home with them. It was my duty. Can I trust you with one of my family's greatest secrets, Erica?" Her face was grave and her eyes didn't waver from her former lover's.

Erica bit back a few more responses and thought about it through the numb cloud currently filling her mind. Even if she suspected Rashida was now as crazy as the letter writer, who would she tell? Her bridge club? Her publisher? Not likely. Besides, how different could this story be from anything she'd read recently? There was even a cat in it. She shrugged and sat down at the table. "Disclose away." She sipped at her tea and waited.

Rashida stood and closed all the blinds and curtains, shrouding the room in twilight gloom. Then she walked over to the table and the cat. She raised her hands to shoulder height and a distant look crossed her features, as if she traveled across time. Her lips parted to emit a chant in a language that Erica did not recognize, one that was at once guttural and musical. The hairs stood up on Erica's nape and she shivered despite herself, filled with a heretofore unknown sense of eldritch dread.

Rashida's eyes were pools of molten gold, her face that of a warrior goddess of old. Erica could not tear her gaze away, though her heart cried out in fear that this new Rashida could never be hers again. The statue's eyes began to glow as the hieroglyphics on its sides were outlined in light. A strange humming sound filled the room, vibrating its way through Erica's china cabinet. The hieroglyphs blazed brilliantly, far too bright to look at, and Erica threw her arm over her face.

The humming lasted a moment more before dying away into silence, and the room went dark once again. "It's safe to look now." Rashida's voice was reassuring but Erica still hesitated a moment before lowering her arm. The cat's inscrutable emerald eyes glowed back at her.

She found her voice with an effort. "So does it do anything besides glow and hum?"

Rashida gave her a look of disbelief. "Of course it does. It's an object of destiny, a source of ancient and terrible power."

"Okay. So what does it actually do?" Erica was beginning to remember one of Rashida's less desirable traits, namely a tendency toward the unnecessarily dramatic.

"It can be used as a weapon of awesome destructive power. And it can bring back what was lost and change destinies, perhaps even raising the dead if the user is powerful enough."

Or it could just be battery-powered and you might be a few scarabs shy of a full complement. Erica stopped the words before they escaped her lips, focusing instead on Rashida's first statement. "What do you mean 'it can be used as a weapon'? What kind of weapon? Used by whom?"

"Only the followers of Set himself, clearly nothing you'd be worried about." Rashida glared at her and Erica realized that she had been using the same voice she used on Mrs. Grayson, her neighbor who had early onset Alzheimer's. "Very well," Rashida said finally. "I can see that you don't believe me. I'll take the statue and go. I have one last task to perform in Foggy Harbor, then we need never see each other again."

"No, wait. What are you going to do next? At least let me cook dinner for you before you go. For old time's sake." Perhaps she could find a way to bring Rashida back to a little of her old, saner self, she thought. Or get her to spend the night. She squelched the second thought.

The doorbell rang again and Erica rolled her eyes. "Let me just get rid of whoever it is and we can have a cozy chat. I'd really like to hear about what you've been up to." *At least I hope I'll like it.* She skirted around the statue as she headed for the front door. No point in taking too many chances. At least it wasn't changing fate right now, and Rashida wasn't bolting for the door.

The doorbell rang again and Erica found herself looking into Alex McGillicuddy's faded blue eyes through the glass pane. She could have screamed with frustration. Instead she made herself open the door. "Hello, Mr. McGillicuddy. I'm afraid I can't stop to chat. I have a guest. Did you need something?" *Such as a shove off my porch?* She held the words back. Clearly Rashida's return was doing nothing for her good nature.

"Well, hello there, neighbor. I didn't mean to intrude -- I was just hoping to get that recipe from you again, the one for that wonderful chicken dish you dropped off when I moved in. I seem to have misplaced the copy you gave me. But it can wait. I've got a frozen pot pie I can just heat up." Alex gave her a look of pure longing that nearly made Erica roll her eyes before he turned away, shoulders slumped with rejection.

Damn the man. "Wait a minute, Alex. We can't have you resorting to the microwave every night. Just follow me back to the kitchen and I'll give you another copy of the recipe." She ushered him, trying not to cringe at his beaming smile.

That was the moment when Rashida emerged from the study. Erica couldn't help the tremor that went through her. After all, Rashida still thought… "Hello. I'm Rashida Simmons," she announced before Erica could say anything. "I understand that congratulations are in order." She gave Alex a stiff, wooden smile and clutched his hand in a death grip, white knuckles clearly visible.

Alex looked surprisingly alert, if a bit baffled. "How do you do? I was just stopping by for a recipe. Congratulations, you say?"

Rashida chose that moment to twist their hands so that Alex's wrist was exposed. Erica caught a brief glimpse of a snakelike tattoo before he yanked his arm away and pulled his sleeve down. Rashida and Alex glared at each other as if they were about to engage in mortal combat.

Desperate to end the standoff, Erica began to babble. "Let's talk about that later, Alex. Rashida and I were just going to sit down to dinner and chat about old times. Why don't we head back to the kitchen so you can get on with your own dinner?" She seized Alex's arm and steered him down the hallway with unnecessary force.

She couldn't help but notice the glance he sent after Rashida as she receded down the hallway in the distance. Had he always possessed that gleam of pure malice in his faded blue eyes? It made her think of ancient temples, their walls oozing with ichor and unspeakable evil. The thought made her scowl fiercely at him. He blinked innocently back, which made her scowl more.

She snatched her recipe box from the stove and yanked the card from the front. "Here you go. Just copy it over and give it back to me when you get around to it. Have a lovely evening!"

She flung her back door open and gave him a smile that contained no ambiguities whatsoever.

"Your friend seems very nice and of course I don't mean to intrude, but perhaps we could all dine together. She seems as though she'd be very interesting to talk to." Alex smiled ingratiatingly at her and made no move toward the door.

"Perhaps another time. We have a lot to catch up on. Now, if you'll excuse me…" Erica glanced pointedly from the door to her neighbor.

At a glacial pace, he stepped toward the door, mumbling words like "sorry" and "intrude." Erica smiled and nodded, making it clear that her mind was somewhere else entirely. Finally, after what seemed an eternity, he oozed out of her kitchen. She watched him make his way down the garden path and out the gate with a fierce enthusiasm.

Then she raced back to the study. An empty room met her eyes: both the statue and Rashida were gone. Erica delivered herself of several unladylike comments before she noticed the note at the edge of the desk. As she reached for it, a part of her could not help but notice that the room felt better somehow. There was no sense of dread, eldritch or otherwise, only her familiar comfortable furniture and her sleeping cats. She glanced at them as if hoping for answers, but only got gentle snores in response.

She opened the note, knowing what it would say. Rashida was gone for good, driven away by some nonsensical quest and the stupid lie that Erica had told her. In a moment of stunning clarity, she recognized that perhaps even a somewhat unhinged Rashida was worth having, at least to her, and she knew despair even before she began reading. The actual text only confirmed her fears.

Dear Erica,

I'm sorry to have intruded on you like this. I had forgotten how people's lives change. Please know that I wish only the best for you in your future life and rest assured that I will not burden you again.

Yours,
Rashida

Erica was just slumping into the chair Rashida had recently occupied when she remembered something that the other woman had said. Something about "one last task." Where could the long lost scion of Nubian priests guarding a sacred relic perform a task here in Foggy Harbor? She wouldn't have gone back to the old Simmons place, surely. Mr. Simmons had passed on a few years back and the family who bought the place had done a drastic remodeling job. That left his old office and...Mrs. Simmon's mausoleum! Of course, why hadn't it occurred to her before?

Erica leapt to her feet and threw caution to the winds. She grabbed her purse and her shoes. Following some instinct she hadn't known she possessed, she bolted down the hall to the kitchen and obtained a small flashlight and, after a moment of hesitation, a box of matches, several packages of salt, and a longish kitchen knife.

Had there been anyone to ask her why she chose those items, she would not have been able to answer them. Perhaps it was one of her own ancestors advising her, maybe a long forgotten Goodie Somebody or Other who narrowly avoiding meeting her death in Salem. Or perhaps it just was editing too many cat horror anthologies. But whatever the reason, the knife felt good and comforting in her hand and the rest felt like essential tools.

She seized her coat from the hook and made sure the cats had enough to eat in case she was gone for a while. The bridge club would take them in if need be, she reminded herself sternly. Then she was off like a shot on her bicycle, peddling as if her life depended on it toward the Shady Oaks Resting Place out on the edge of town. Rashida would be there already, if that's where she was headed. Erica hoped for the best and rode as she had never ridden before.

Fortunately, the cemetery was not far away and traffic was light. Erica skidded to a halt in front of the locked gates moments later and wondered how she was going to get inside. Then she remembered that Rashida had another way in, a gap in the fence some ways down that she used when she wanted to visit the family tomb after hours. She rode her bike on a bit further, then chained it to a post near where she thought the hole was.

With a deep breath, she straightened out her coat and marched up to the fence. Her memory had served her well. An impossibly skinny opening met her searching gaze and she despaired. Then she heard the noise of an engine, one that sounded vaguely threatening, if an engine could be described that way. She shrank into the shadows and glanced around.

Alex was parking his car on the street near the cemetery entrance. And he wasn't alone. There were two men with him, neither of them familiar, but both of an aspect that would have caused a braver heart than Erica's to quail. They got out of the car and made for the locked gates of the cemetery.

For an instant, she thought of going home and calling the police. But what would she tell them? Then she thought of the way Alex had looked at Rashida when they met. There had been something in his expression that filled her with urgency. She found that if she held her breath and twisted just right, she was able to squeeze through the fence to fall, gasping, onto the soft green grass on the other side.

She could hear an ominous clicking noise from the entrance; they must be cutting or picking the lock. Brushing herself off, she rose and sprinted for the deeper shadows under the trees. Then she pulled out her little flashlight, and shielding it as much as she could with her fingers, she dashed forward through the tombstones and trees toward the Simmons mausoleum.

It took longer than she expected and she got lost once, but she finally found it. To the amazement of Foggy Harbor, Rashida's grandfather had built the family tomb as a small stone pyramid in the midst of the more standard marble structures. It was trimmed with black stone and guarded by statues of Anubis and Bastet. There were even hieroglyphs, which everyone else in town thought was an unbearable pretension. Erica had thought so herself upon occasion. Now her nerves were so agitated, it was all she could do to approach the structure.

As she got closer, she noticed that the hieroglyphs were glowing faintly. Could Rashida be inside, unaware of her danger? Still, she mustn't overreact. She couldn't be absolutely sure that Alex presented any kind of threat. Perhaps he just enjoyed late night visits to cemeteries with large male friends. Large terrifying male friends.

Erica squared her shoulders and tried to remember where the catch for the door was hidden. Then she reached into the recess next to the door and opened it. The mechanism still worked flawlessly after all these years. Without stopping to marvel at that minor miracle, she slipped inside and let it click shut behind her.

She had expected to walk into Stygian gloom but to her surprise, the interior was lit with a pale golden glow. It was bright enough to illuminate the names on the memorials, including those of Rashida's parents. Erica wondered who, if anyone, was buried in her mother's tomb before she turned away, shivering a bit.

In the middle of the floor, one of the great marble slabs was pulled aside and a flight of steps led downward. From below, she thought she could hear the sound of muted chanting, and it sent chills up her already frozen spine. She considered demanding that Rashida stop all this nonsense and come upstairs to talk to her, but the words would not cross her immobile lips.

Instead, Erica closed her eyes and remembered Rashida as she had been, back when they were first together at Foggy Harbor State, before that first fateful Egyptology class. She caressed the memory of Rashida's golden eyes in the sunset and the way she felt when—she made herself stop and shuffle toward the steps. There would be time for trips down Memory Lane later, once all this was over. Alex and his thugs could only be minutes behind her.

Even so she crept down the stairs at a snail's pace. The sight that met her eyes when she reached the bottom was not one that even her books could have prepared her for. Rashida stood before an altar presided over by the cat statue. The air was thick with incense and the smoke of many candles. Her former lover was naked to the waist, though she still wore her gray wool pants. Above those, she was clad only in massive gold jewelry: a collar, several arm rings, huge earrings. She raised a blood-covered knife as she chanted. Erica could see shallow gashes in her arms, and the sight made her shudder all over.

Rashida was completely unaware of her, her golden eyes rimmed with kohl and focused on another world. Erica shrank back for a moment, too terrified to approach her friend. She could see that there was a dish of blood in front of the statue and for a ghastly moment, she feared that her friend had come to sacrifice herself to the mysterious statue. That thought was enough to break through her fears. “No!” She cried, her voice cutting through the smoke and the chanting like a blade.

Rashida faltered, and Erica could feel the air of the chamber tense and coil, becoming suddenly dangerous to the point of madness. Something unfathomably evil lurked there, somehow, just outside the realm of human senses. Using all of her strength, Erica leaped forward and pulled Rashida to the floor, knocking the knife from her hands and covering her with her trembling body in a vain effort to protect her.

It was at that moment Alex and his minions burst into the tomb. They thundered downstairs just as Erica thought the air itself was about to strike them all down. Alex laughed, a cold mirthless sound in the murk of the chamber. “It seems you received a package intended for me, Guardian.” He stepped forward, towering over them, his eyes cold and clearer than Erica had ever seen them.

Well, she thought, somewhat hysterically, *if it's just a post office mix-up, we can all go home. No harm done.* Her glance fell on one of the men with Alex and she was quiet. Harm would be done tonight and it was only a matter of time before it was clear who would be the recipient of it.

Rashida stirred from underneath her, easing Erica off to one side. “It is not for you, oh Servant of Set! It is my sacred mission to guard it and guard it I shall,” Rashida's lips were set, a deep fury burning in her eyes. She had not yet looked at Erica, but the latter was not looking forward to the moment when her attention shifted.

She had to cut the tension somehow. “Really, Alex, if I'd know you had such an interest in antiquities, I'd have gone to the museum with you when you asked. Perhaps we can continue this discussion over dinner?” Erica asked hopefully.

"Let her go, she knows nothing about this." Rashida's eyes never left Alex's.

"On the contrary, she has some suspicions about me. And she is curious enough that it is only a matter of time before she wants to know more. Isn't that right, my dear?" Alex gave Erica a mock flirtatious leer that made her grimace in disgust.

Alex McGillicuddy is a minion of Set? Hard to believe. At least at first, but when she thought about it more, it gave her some perspective on the attentions he'd been showing her. Clearly she was better off single. Not that that was her biggest concern at the moment.

Whoever or whatever Alex was, he was annoying her greatly right now. She said the most outrageous thing she could think of. "That's it. The wedding's off." She glared at Alex and scrambled to her feet as Rashida did the same. The air around them seemed to have thinned a bit, as if the chanting had stopped calling whatever it was bringing into this world from one beyond.

Alex looked baffled. "The wedd—oh, never mind." His gaze fell on the statue and his eyes brightened with dark emotions. "Take the cat, boys, and we'll just seal up our little friends in their tomb. I'm sure they can comfort each other for a while, at least until the air runs out."

"Wait," Rashida held up her hand. "This is not your Lord's. Its powers will not obey you." Erica could feel a force coiling around them again, could feel something coming to a summons she could not hear. She reached into her handbag and found the packets of salt. As slowly and carefully as she could, she pulled them out. She glanced sidelong at Rashida and noticed that the latter seemed to be preparing to attack Alex.

The cat glowed even brighter as one of the thugs approached it. Alex hadn't answered Rashida's challenge, which was not surprising, since his attention seemed wholly fixed on the statue. But he had a gun out now and was pointing it at them.

Erica reached into her bag with excruciating slowness and pulled out the knife. She handed it to Rashida who gave her a bemused but still angry glance. "Athame," Erica muttered as softly as she could, using the only word she could remember from *Kitties in the Witch House*, her very nearly best-selling anthology.

Rashida smiled and it was an expression that made her face beautiful and terrible all at once. Following the strange instinct that had driven her since she left the house, Erica tore open the packets of salt and threw their contents out around them in a rough circle. "Hold it!" Alex barked at them just as his minion touched the cat.

The air above the altar grew dark as Rashida began to chant again. It swirled around the man, something glowing in its depths that Erica could not bear to look at. She closed her eyes and ducked as a bullet from Alex's gun whizzed past. The words flowing from Rashida's lips were like the ones she'd been chanting when Erica first entered, but they were different in timbre somehow. She was still terrified but she felt protected, as if whatever powers Rashida was calling were no longer harmful. At least to them.

A high-pitched, piercing cry of utter pain and terror filled the room. Erica covered her ears and flinched away and even Rashida stumbled in her chant. The air thickened and tightened above the altar, reminding Erica of nothing so much as a giant serpent. Or a very sinuous cat. Alex's henchman waved his arms and flailed as if trying to fend off some invisible foe. Then with a scream horrific in its finality, he fell to the floor, motionless.

Alex trained his gun on Rashida. "Call it off, witch. Your creature can't kill me before I fire this again." His eyes were icy in the murk of the chamber, even though his remaining thug shook with fear at his side.

Erica gave Rashida a panicked look. She couldn't lose her now, not like this. Rashida laughed, the rich mellow sound filling the chamber around them. The thing above the altar hovered, its face taking shape and growing pointed ears. The face hovered above the bowl of Rashida's blood, a ghastly phantom tongue lapping at its contents. Rashida glanced at it before meeting Alex's eyes. "Bets?" She inquired in a somewhat bored voice.

Erica's eyes widened in horror as she saw Alex's finger tighten on the trigger, then change his mind and point the gun at her. Rashida whispered something that might have been a prayer or a curse. She brought the kitchen knife down in a slashing moment as Alex pulled the trigger. A white cloud rose from the circle of salt around them and Erica watched as the bullet slowed to a crawl, stopping inches from her shoulder. Rashida reached out and flicked it with her finger, sending it to roll on the floor.

Alex's eyes narrowed and his thin lips parted in a chant of his own. Rashida gestured, and the cloud edged closer to his remaining minion. The man stood his ground a moment, then glanced at his fallen comrade, and fled up the stairs. The cloud appeared to have grown paws now, and it circled Alex, a glow that might have been eyes fixed on his upraised hands.

The sounds that fell from Alex's lips were cold and cruel, an ancient evil walking among them. Erica nearly covered her eyes before deciding that she couldn't bear not to watch. A second shadow arose from the cat statue, this one clearly a serpent with a fiery eyes. The cat shadow turned toward it, its spectral mouth opened in a silent hiss.

Then the two were joined in battle as their acolytes chanted at each other across the tomb. Erica glanced from one to the other, wondering what, if anything, she should do. The circle of salt still glowed faintly around them, which was reassuring. She watched the shadows battle for a moment and considered whether or not to simply sit down and wait it out. But that seemed cowardly somehow.

Rashida's face looked strained when she glanced back, and a new sense of urgency filled Erica at the sight. She wondered if she could learn an ancient chant in the next minute or two and help that way, but languages had never been her forte. Next she speculated that there might be something she could do to help the shadow kitty win its battle, but that too seemed unlikely.

Then she looked up at Alex. He seemed stronger, his face twisted in an expression of pure evil. He was also closer than she'd realized, only a few feet away from the edge of their protective circle. There didn't seem to be much time left. A deus ex machina did not seem forthcoming.

It was then that Erica had an idea. It was a weird sort of idea, but she thought it just might work. She reached into her purse and took out her book of matches. Then she took off her sweater and wrapped it around her fake leather purse. She lit several matches and with only the slightest of qualms, she held the sputtering flame to her favorite sweater. As the wool caught on fire, she studied the distance between them and Alex with narrowed eyes.

When at last she made her throw, she threw it underhand, just 'like a girl' as Rashida would have said in disgust back when they played college softball. She lobbed it with care and skill, though, and no one could argue with the results. The ball of flaming wool and plastic landed at Alex's feet, sparks catching on his pants. He hesitated, his chant faltering for a breath, then two, as he stamped and shook his feet to put out the flames that engulfed his cuffs.

With a hiss that knocked Erica to her knees, the cat shadow found some hidden source of strength. When she looked up, she could see the serpent dangling from its spectral kitty jaws. She looked at Rashida, hoping to see that her friend had found the same strength. But to her horror, Rashida seemed nearly spent.

A loud noise distracted her, and she looked at Alex in time to see him drop his gun. She gathered herself and hopped out of the salt circle. Immediately, mighty forces assailed her and she walked forward as if in a gale. But walk forward she did until she was able to reach the gun. She managed to pick it up and hold it out in front of her with hands that shook convulsively. "All right," she said in a voice that shook nearly as badly. "Enough of this nonsense."

She pointed the gun in Alex's general direction and pulled the trigger, the recoil knocking her to the floor. Her shot missed, but it was enough to make him flinch. Rashida's words fell like hail, faster and more powerful, than before and Alex dropped to his knees, hands pressed over his ears, silent at last. A great rushing sound tore through the chamber and both cat and serpent vanished. The glow of the hieroglyphs faded until only the candles and the fiery sweater still provided light.

Rashida stepped forward and raised the kitchen knife above Alex, her face transformed into the countenance of a goddess of death. "No!" Erica shouted.

Her friend seemed to shift, as if another person was working their way to the surface. "I know you were engaged to him and all, but really Erica, I'm sure you can see he's not the greatest catch."

Erica's jaw dropped open. "I was never engaged to him! I just said that because I was angry with you. That's no reason to kill him." She staggered to her feet. "You won't call on powerful dark forces from beyond this world again, will you, Mr. McGillicuddy?"

Alex hissed something that might have been agreement. His eyes were dead now, as if the spirit which drove him was gone. Looking into them, Erica had another idea. "Besides, maybe he knows what happened to your mother."

Rashida's face shifted, becoming more Rashida again. "Do you, Set-spawn? Do you know something?" She waved the knife threateningly in front of his dazed looking face.

It seemed to be enough to bring him back to life, and his lips twisted in a snarl. "My Lord consumed her, body and spirit, just as he will consume you!" Then he twisted around and kicked out with desperate strength. Rashida jumped back as he pulled himself to his feet. Then he charged forward, straight at the cat on the altar. Rashida lunged after him, but not quickly enough, as he darted past her and placed his hands on the statue.

For a moment, nothing happened. His face twisted and it seemed to Erica as if he was drawing on some unseen source of power. The statue began to glow a little, then a bit more. A tendril of shadow reached out from it and wrapped itself around his body in a hideously companionable fashion. He threw back his head and laughed, and the shadow slipped into his mouth. His laughter changed to a choking cough and he fell to the floor, his body convulsing, until just as suddenly, he was still.

The statue fell with him, meeting the stone floor with a crash. The head broke loose and shadows poured out. They surged out in a mighty gray wave, then just as quickly dissipated. In their wake, they left two corpses and two exhausted women. "Well, looks like that might be it for your task," Erica said in awed but relieved tones.

Rashida stared at her in disbelief, then picked her way across the floor to the statue. She picked up the head and held it as if seeking answers to questions only she could hear. The green eyes twinkled in the cat's face but volunteered nothing. A single tear worked its way down Rashida's cheek.

Erica ran over to comfort her. She wrapped her arms around her friend and held her tightly, and in that brief instant, both of them touched the cat. The statue quivered and shook, light pouring from it instead of shadows this time. It engulfed them, then swept through the chamber and up the stairs into the mausoleum. Then it too vanished as the shadows had done.

"We've released all that it held," Rashida whispered. "There is nothing more to guard."

Erica kissed her bare shoulder and turned her around so she could kiss the tears from her cheeks. "Where are the rest of your clothes, by the way?"

Rashida pointed up wordlessly. Erica took the pieces of the statue and tucked them into her capacious pockets. Then she took Rashida's hand in hers and towed her along as she walked over to pick her house keys out of the smoldering wreckage of her purse. "Let's go home and eat dinner." She smiled reassuringly at Rashida, but the latter seemed lost in her thoughts.

Erica pulled her up the stairs behind her. There was a faint knocking coming from Keira Simmons' tomb. They looked at each other, and Erica shrugged and nodded, the experiences of the evening having completely exhausted her capacity for terror. Rashida pulled on her shirt and jacket before they approached the tomb. They looked deep into each other's eyes for a long moment, then they pushed the lid away. Keira Simmons sat up, clearly alive, her face that of someone waking from a long sleep.

"Hello Mother," Rashida choked out at last. "I asked Bastet to help me find you, and she has." Rashida burst into tears.

Erica nodded politely to Mrs. Simmons as she and her daughter tearfully embraced. She gave Rashida a wan smile before turning and walking out of the tomb. She had no place in this part of Rashida's story. Still, she ached at the thought that she might never see Rashida again. In an acute state of emotional turmoil, she retrieved her bike, and went home where she tumbled into bed and slept for many hours.

She was sitting at her kitchen table the next morning reading stories with titles like "Kittens in the Walls" when the doorbell rang. Once more she shuffled slowly down the hall but this time she flung the door open without bothering to see who it was first.

Rashida looked back at her, golden eyes calm and peaceful. "I was thinking," she said without preamble, "that I missed you." Then she stepped up and took the astonished Erica in her arms for a long kiss. And Erica kissed her back, right there on the doorstep in front of all of Foggy Harbor. Then she took Rashida's hand and pulled her inside, shutting the door behind her.

The Letter of Marque

Celeste Adéle Gírard laughed, fluttering her fan just below her topaz eyes. The gesture was enough to make her audience, old rakes and young chevaliers alike, vie against each other even harder to make her laugh again. But Celeste was becoming distracted. Her gaze turned as often on the ballroom door as it did to her admirers, making their aspirations even more difficult to attain.

A liveried footman announced each new guest as they arrived, bowing them into the Governor's ballroom as if it were Versailles itself. Celeste smothered a sigh at the memory of her last vision of her beloved France. Oh, to leave this benighted island, hot, dull and filled with boorish Englishmen!

Sternly, she reminded herself that the King had promised to make her a Countess if she succeeded in her mission. That alone should be reason enough to stay. She drew herself up and smiled harder.

It was at that moment the footman announced a "Mr. Bernard." Mademoiselle Gírard merely glanced briefly toward the door as if the arrival of the man she hunted was of little moment before declaring herself faint from the heat. A hundred arms, or so it seemed, were proffered and she was soon swept off to an elegant, uncomfortable chair from which she could observe her quarry. The youngest of her admirers was dispatched to fetch her wine and exited with resigned grace.

Bernard had not seen her, which was as well since he might have recognized her from the Court. But he spared none of the young ladies present a glance on his way across the room to the Governor's side. Sir Henry Morgan, Governor of His Majesty's colony of Jamaica, seemed inclined to both welcome and listen to the gentleman. Certainly their faces were serious enough to suggest grave matters, and that alone was unusual on such an occasion.

"La!" Celeste murmured. "It is so hot in here. Perhaps you would be so kind as to escort me?" She gestured toward the open balcony at Morgan's back and fluttered her lids at the young man who had just returned with her wine. His youthful cheeks flushed crimson but he was fast enough to offer his hand to assist her in standing, moving with a fencer's grace before the others could reach out.

He was swift enough too in sweeping her over the floor and out into the relative cool of the deserted night air before anyone could follow. Celeste gave him a speculative glance. There was not even the beginning of a beard on his tanned cheeks. But his expression, now that suggested years of a certain kind of experience she would not have expected in one so young. Had she miscalculated? She had thought him easily handled. Celeste frowned a moment, slightly puzzled.

The young man murmured in near perfect court French, "How lovely you are tonight, mademoiselle." He reached out and twirled one of her blonde curls around his finger, barely grazing the bare skin of her neck in what was clearly a deliberate gesture.

Celeste shivered despite herself. He moved his hand up and traced the delicate shell of her ear. "And such perfect ears, straining so very hard to hear the English Governor's words.

What do they talk about inside, do you think, the former pirate and the French gentleman in the somber clothes?"

He had leaned over so that his lips were nearly at her ear and this time, Celeste did start. She stared up at him in the moonlight, her eyes narrowed in suspicion. "Who are you?"

"Another lost soul from France, my lady." The words were said with a smile that sent Celeste's fingers searching for the small dagger hidden in her skirts. The young man caught her hand and pressed it to his lips. "Surely so beautiful a flower has nothing to fear from a boy like me?"

Now Celeste did stare. What was it about this lad? He had a pretty face, did the young man, with a long, narrow jaw, brown eyes, and a thin patrician nose, all beneath a shock of dark red hair. She dropped her gaze to his beardless chin and from there, below. "Mon dieu! You're a woman!" She gasped at last.

The young man went on holding her hand. "Captain Jacquotte Delahaye, at your service."

"The pir--!" Jacquotte's fingers were on her lips now, silencing her startled exclamation. Celeste could feel her eyes go round, like a girl scarcely out of the nursery and she despised herself for it. With an effort, she squelched her awe.

Even though she stood in the moonlight with the celebrated French pirate queen, steps away, an Englishman plotted against the French King. There was no time for this nonsense. Her expression must have changed because the pirate pulled her fingers away, so speedily she must have feared being bitten.

Celeste pushed her companion back toward the curtain, a low, flirtatious laugh rising from her lips. "Oh sir," she said with an excellent English accent, "You are too forward!"

Delahaye smiled and looked down at her as if she was the only maiden in the world. The Governor and Mr. Bernard continued their discourse. Now and then, a word, a phrase, drifted out on the night breeze. There was mention of a treasure, then something else she could not hear.

A moment later, though, Morgan's voice boomed out, "You have done well, Sir. Come to my residence tomorrow and we will discuss payment." The Governor slapped his guest on the shoulder, clearly to the other man's distaste, and turned to survey the room. His expression was shrewd as he glanced around, pausing a moment on the two figures on the balcony.

"Don't bite me, chéri," Jacquotte murmured a moment before Celeste found herself being thoroughly kissed. She pushed vainly against the pirate's muscular arms and shoulders but could do nothing against being held tight in the other woman's grasp. It was only for a few breathless seconds, but it was enough to her gasping for air and filled with strange sensations. Delahaye released her. "Now behave as you would with any young man who took such liberties."

Celeste slapped her hard. "How dare you, sir! I am not to be used in this way." She shoved Jacquotte so that she stumbled back, releasing her grip. Then she stormed into the ballroom in time to catch Governor Morgan's eye.

The old pirate leered and offered his arm. "And how could any man resist stealing a kiss from such beauty? Permit me, my dear. I shall keep you safe at my side until you desire otherwise. You are newly come from England to visit Lady Aston, are you not?"

Celeste noticed that Monsieur Bernard had vanished as suddenly as he had come. She simpered and blushed under the Governor's eye, summoning nearly forgotten skills. The blush was long out of fashion in Paris, but here it seemed required. "Yes, my Lord. Jamaica is such a beautiful island!"

Morgan smiled down at her, while his black eyes caressed her décolletage so that if she had been the maid she pretended to be, she might have feared for her virtue. As it was, she thought of her mission, and not a little of Jacquotte Delahaye. With the former in mind, she prattled on about the tropics and about her fear of pirates, now assuaged by the presence of such a stalwart representative of His Majesty's government.

At the mention of pirates, Morgan's face changed from flirtatious to stone. Celeste found herself transferred inelegantly from the Governor's arm to that of Lady Aston, who approached at his gesture. "He's very sensitive on that topic, my dear," Lady Aston murmured as the Governor stomped off.

Celeste very nearly rolled her eyes. Lady Aston was charming, of course, but sometimes that was simply not enough. Just then, their progress toward the door was blocked by a familiar figure.

"Monsieur Lafitte, Madam, at your service. My apologies, Lady Aston. I feel I must beg forgiveness from your young charge." Jacquotte Delahaye made a sweeping bow, graceful and powerful. "I was overcome by the moonlight, beautiful lady. Please forgive me. Say that I may call on you tomorrow."

Celeste drew back, her heart pounding. Whatever the pirate wanted here, it could have nothing to do with her. Unless she too sought the Spanish gold that the King of France needed? There was only one way to find out. She might yet prove useful as well as intriguing. Celeste fluttered her fan once more as if undecided. Lady Aston sounded puzzled as she answered for them both, "I'm not sure what you mean, sir." She studied Celeste askance as if wondering what mischief her young charge had gotten into.

"Very well. You may call tomorrow afternoon." Celeste closed her fan with a snap and tugged Lady Aston forward. Delahaye stepped back and they made their escape.

Lady Aston looked both amused and concerned as they entered her coach. "Have you acquired an admirer, my dear?"

"Something even better." Celeste's smile was more genuine than it had been all evening, but not another word would she say on the topic. Instead she steered her friend into the safer waters of gossip and fashion. Such things were far less likely to place her neck in a noose than knowing the secrets of the King of France's best spy in the Caribbean.

Celeste's mind was whirling when she reached her room, and once her maid had unlaced her and helped her into her nightdress, she found herself dismissed. Her mistress paced the room as she left, absently running a brush through her blonde curls.

Morgan and his mysterious visitor had to have been speaking about the missing treasure of Jean Fleury. Rumors that the privateer's gold had finally been discovered, possibly by Bernard himself, had drifted as far as Versailles and the King's ear. And here she was, sent to find the truth. She pulled her orders and papers from their hiding place and spread them on the desk. But she wasn't ready to sit down and read through them again, not yet.

She had managed to gain enough information in the last fortnight to make it clear that the stories were true, but as to the who and the where of it, that was more challenging. For that, she would need something more than her disguise as an English near-innocent come to visit her aunt in Jamaica. She opened the wardrobe and reached into its darkest recesses. There was a click, as of a tiny secret lock, then she emerged carrying a bundle of clothes, a pair of boots and a sheathed sword.

The curtains at the open window fluttered, their white length startling her. But that was nothing in comparison to her response to the appearance of Jacquotte Delahaye in their midst. "Good evening, mademoiselle. I prefer to set my own hours for visiting." The pirate smiled.

Celeste threw the clothes and boots aside and drew the sword with the ease of long practice. She held the length of her rapier between herself and her unexpected visitor. “What are you doing here?”

The pirate looked amused. “I’m accustomed to young ladies shrieking for their maids when I appear in their rooms. This is something new. But then, you’re not what you seem, are you, mademoiselle?”

“Do you make a habit of sneaking into ladies’ bedrooms at night then? I though pirates sailed on ships and robbed on the high seas.” Inwardly, Celeste cursed Delahaye’s timing. A few more minutes and she would have been dressed for fighting. Now, her nightdress would slow her down. But she did not let the pirate see that thought and the hand that held the rapier was rock steady.

“Only very unusual young ladies.” Delahaye nodded toward the sword. “I can see that you can handle your blade from your stance. So now that I know that, put up your sword, lass. I’ve come to talk.”

“Talk fast then. My aunt often comes to my room to say good night.”

Delahaye moved like a striking cat, knocking aside Celeste’s blade with a pillow she seized on her way to the door. With a single gesture, she slid the bolt home and leaned against it. “Now we won’t be disturbed.” She looked around the room, ignoring Celeste’s muffled curse as she rubbed her wrist. “Ah. Just what I was looking for.” She snatched the papers from the writing desk and drew her pistol, pointing it at Celeste.

Celeste saw her death in its round mouth for a span of breaths. But Delahaye did not pull the trigger. Instead, she rifled through the papers as if looking for something specific. Celeste lunged forward, hoping to catch her off guard.

Delahaye spun away, her expression annoyed. She leveled the pistol at Celeste's head and spoke in a tone that did not allow for disagreement. "Do that again, mademoiselle, and I'll be forced to damage a work of art."

Then she seemed to find what she was seeking. She studied the document with a satisfied expression that froze Celeste in place, waiting for what she could not prevent. She read aloud, "It is in the service of the King of France that the bearer of this letter has done what she has done." Delahaye's smile turned wicked. "You have a landsman's letter of marque, mademoiselle. Perhaps you might tell me why."

The pirate's dark eyes were cold and fierce and the easy lie she had been about to tell caught in Celeste's throat. What would Delahaye believe? The pirate continued, "I'll make it simple for you then. You are a Frenchwoman pretending to be English and you can handle a sword. I believe you to be either a spy or an assassin. Now what has Sir Henry Morgan got that your King Louis wants?"

"He is your King as well as mine," Celeste retorted, her tone ice in the humid air. "Now put my papers back. I would dislike to add you to my list of enemies, Mon—Mademoiselle." She stumbled over the words, wincing at her own clumsiness.

Jacquotte Delahaye laughed softly. "Madame, if you will. But alas, widowed."

"Widowed? By your own hand, no doubt! Never mind." Celeste gestured. "I have no wish to know the fate of Monsieur Delahaye. I do, however, want my papers back and to be free of your presence."

"And thus I am dismissed." Jacquotte crossed the room, pistol still pointed steadily at Celeste. She seated herself on the edge of the bed. "Sit," she gestured at the room's only chair.

Celeste gritted her teeth. "I prefer to stand."

"Indeed." Jacquotte shrugged. "Well, mademoiselle, I have speculated on your purpose here in Jamaica and you have not denied my theories."

"Do you really believe me an assassin?"

"I imagine that I would even now be fighting for my life if that were the case." Jacquotte's eyes gleamed with mockery. "I suspect that we both seek the same goal, however: Jean Fleury's gold. Though it would seem we have a different purpose for its use."

Celeste snorted. "The taverns of Port Royal are hardly a noble purpose."

"In comparison to gold-plating the asses of some aristocrats at Versailles? No, I suppose not. In any case, I desire more than that and you, mademoiselle, may help me achieve what I desire. I am willing to divide the gold equally in return for your help."

"And if I don't wish to help you?" It was an extraordinary offer. Extraordinary and ridiculous. Why should this woman think she would accept it?

"I could shoot you now," Jacquotte responded, her expression thoughtful. "But that would rouse the household and be something of a waste. No, mademoiselle, refuse my generosity and I will foil your plans at every turn. Consider, if you will, that I have a ship and men at my command. You have only your wits and considerable charms. How will you liberate the gold? What will you do with it then?"

Celeste studied the pirate before answering. It seemed wisest to appear as foolish as the other woman thought her. She mustered a look of confusion. "I can call upon any French ship in these waters."

"Then as you have been so eager to declare me a subject of the King of France, allow me to offer my ship as the one you call upon. Provided, of course, that you accede to my wishes."

"Which I know nothing of. Do you plan to enlighten me?"

"It will be nothing beyond your powers, I can assure you. Now I have other business to attend to and must take my leave." Jacquotte stood, but clearly waited for a response.

Celeste frowned as if considering her options. Finally, she summoned a reluctant, "Very well."

"Excellent. Then I will take my leave, Celeste, if I may call you so, and leave you to your dreams." The pirate vanished out the window before Celeste was able to respond.

She dashed over and looked out. Delahaye was clambering down the vines on the wall below, ending with a short leap into the bushes. She was gone from view within moments, leaving her audience shivering behind her. Celeste closed the window before she turned back to the room.

Within moments, she was dressed in her man's garb. She buckled her rapier to her belt, slid daggers into the sheaths in the top of her boots and bound up her hair so it would tuck up beneath her hat. The heavy vest that she added next would leave her panting if she had to run but would cover her breasts enough so that she might pass as a man, if not examined too closely. She had no intention of letting anyone get close enough to notice.

Last, she caught up her most important papers and slipped them into a pouch that hung around her neck and tucked it beneath her shirt. They would be safer there, she suspected since Delahaye had entered her room so easily and might well return.

Then she grabbed the rope she had stored in with her clothes and opened the window once more. After securing it to her bedpost, she began her own descent to the ground below. Miraculously, it seemed as if Lady Aston's household slept through it all. She viewed the darkened windows above her with relief. Lady Aston had been so kind, had asked so few questions of the daughter of her former school friend, that to distress her seemed an unkindness.

Celeste slipped through the garden like a shadow, silently traversing her way through the old gate in the far wall and into the quiet streets beyond. The streets of Port Royal were as close to silent as they ever were. Celeste could hear drunken shouts in the distance as she slipped quietly through the darkened streets. She made a right turn, then two lefts then straight until she saw torches flickering feebly before an old inn. Faded letters pronounced it to be "The Sea Dog."

She stepped forward with a quick glance to either side to verify that she was not followed. Then she loosened her sword in its scabbard and opened the tavern door with a manly swagger. Still, her heart raced as she looked around the common room, prepared as she could be, for anything.

Fortunately, the lateness of the hour ensured that there were few within still sober enough to sit upright. Men slept on the benches or head down on the tables. A whore snored in a corner near the unlit fireplace. Only one or two heads turned to watch her, then looked away when they saw her sword. The landlord gave her a hard stare, then jerked his head toward a closed door in the darkened recesses under the stairs when she gave him a two-fingered salute.

She nodded as she slipped under the stairs and rapped the door three times. Responding to a sound from within, she entered. The two men at the table stood, one after the other. The taller one swept his plumed hat from his head and would have bowed had he not been stopped by a preemptory gesture. A few moments of muted conversation followed and candlelight glinted on a handful of gold coins as they changed hands. Then all three left the room, and the tall man tossed the landlord a coin.

Once outside, they separated, each moving in a different direction. Celeste directed her steps back toward Lady Aston's and bed. Perhaps weariness made her careless, or so she thought afterwards. By then it was too late. Before she knew she was under attack, shadowy figures forced a foul-smelling sack over her head and knocked her unconscious.

When she awoke, she was bound hand and foot, but at least the sack was gone. Her head hurt like the very Devil, and she could feel the sea's motion somewhere under the table she was tied to. The room was nearly dark, for which she was grateful given how much her head hurt. She forced herself to test her limbs, then to try her bonds. Both were solid but the movements hurt enough to tear a groan from her throat.

As if it was a signal, a huge man opened the door and stepped inside. He grinned down at her, his smile exposing a few missing teeth. His beard was filthy and his person made even less appealing by the stench that rolled off him: rum and long unwashed flesh.

Celeste yanked frantically at her bonds, nearly breaking her wrists in her struggles. She had sworn that no man would harm her again; two deaths were testament to that vow. But now she was helpless.

The man laughed and stepped closer, meaty hands descending on her bound legs. His fingers dug into her flesh through her breeches. "You're a pretty piece, aren't you? Think I'll have me a bit of fun while the Captain's not about." He leered as his hands slid higher and Celeste cursed him with every oath in her vocabulary.

The door opened behind him with a sharp bang, making them both jump, and she could see another man in the doorway. Silently, she vowed that she would live to kill them all, every one of them. That determination leant steel to her spine and a layer of ice to calm her panic. She had only to endure, wait for her chance and be ready.

A sharp blow from behind staggered the brute and he fell away, spinning around with his knife drawn. He was snarling now, knife held at the ready, knees in a fighter's couch. But there was a sword's point hovering before his eyes now and at the other end, the blazing eyes of Jacquotte Delahaye.

Celeste wondered if she was swordsman enough to defeat an opponent nearly twice her size. She worked even harder at loosening her bonds; after all even if Delahaye won this unequal combat, there was no guarantee that Celeste would not be next.

The clash of blades tore her from her thoughts. The man had lunged at Jacquotte and she had turned his blade easily. The knife blade flashed as he matched her movements, looking for a chance to get past her rapier. But her guard held. "Give it up, Poole," she said in heavily accented English. "Your pigsticker is no match for my steel."

He growled something at her and Celeste could see his free hand dart out of sight, searching for something to hurl. "Watch out!" She exclaimed as his hand closed on a loose bolt.

Jacquotte dodged as it sailed through the air to smash on the wood behind her, then ducked under his arm and drove her sword into his shoulder. He bellowed in pain as she yanked the blade free and pressed the tip against his throat. The knife fell to the floor with a clatter and Celeste smiled as blood began to stain his already filthy coat.

Delahaye raised one dark eyebrow. "Is this done?" Poole nodded. "Disobey me again and I'll cut your balls off and stuff them down your throat." She stepped aside and he sidled past her, clearly reluctant to turn his back until he could stumble away across the deck.

"Now, as to you, mademoiselle, my apologies for your treatment. I anticipated that you might prove...reluctant to cooperate if you had too much time to think." Jacquotte smiled and it sent shivers down Celeste's spine. "But I suppose my point is made." With a few deft turns of her wrist, she severed the ropes that bound her captive to the table.

Celeste sat up awkwardly, hands still bound. She held them out, "What must I exchange for my freedom?"

Jacquotte's smile changed a bit, her lips twisting in a slight grimace. "So simple? I must wonder. But here it is, mademoiselle. I want a letter of my own, one that says that I do what must be done in the service of France. I would like to return home a welcome hero, not a despised pirate. This is my price." Her back straightened and she looked past Celeste as she spoke, as if she was seeing into the future she described.

"A letter of marque, making you a privateer for the King?" Celeste spoke slowly, trying to think. It surprised her that Delahaye would trade the complete freedom of the seas to pillage for France but if the great pirate Henry Morgan could turn governor, anything was possible. "And for this, you will help me to capture all of Fleury's treasure for France?"

"Let us say much of it. I have expenses." Jacquotte sheathed her sword and gestured expansively at the cabin walls.

"Rob more Spanish and English dogs then, and leave the King of France his gold." Celeste growled. "Fleury would have done so had he lived."

"Would he? God save us all from honorable pirates," Jacquotte laughed. "Now, Mademoiselle Celeste, I will free you if I have your word that you will not attempt to slaughter the crew or myself."

"It is much to ask." She could feel the boat's motion changing, as if sails were being brought in. "Where are we?"

"We are following our mysterious countryman, he who is such a good friend of Monsieur the Governor." Jacquotte gestured toward the open door. "Do you wish to see if we have been successful at finding his hiding place?"

Celeste held out her bound hands in mute answer, nodding to the question in Jacquotte's eyes. Her wrists were free a moment later and she was staggering to her feet on legs not yet seaworthy. Jacquotte caught her arm and guided her forward to the door, and from there across the deck.

Despite her stumbling, Celeste was able to look around the ship as they moved toward the prow. It had been a flagship once, probably English, from the build, before it turned pirate. The black flag was folded and stowed on deck, she noticed, while the ship flew merchant colors from Portugal.

But the men were as she expected: a rainbow-hued assortment of cutthroats, murderers and common sailors. Celeste glanced from one scarred or tattooed hard-eyed face to another and wondered what kind of woman could survive their company.

Jacquotte looked at her and smiled as if she had spoken her thoughts aloud. "I'm their Captain and they know I'm fair. Everyone gets an even split of the spoils. It's enough for most of them. The rest know I can kill them and that's enough for the rest."

Celeste felt her lips curl into a reluctant smile. It was difficult not to feel admiration for this pirate. She only hoped that she would not be forced to kill her.

A motion out on the water caught her attention: some distance away, a small boat was sailing into what appeared to be a wall of rock. "Look!" The word fell from her lips before she realized that Jacquotte had released her arm and was now training a spyglass on the ship. "Are we going in after him?" She demanded, her voice full of newfound eagerness for the hunt.

Jacquotte did not lower the glass. "No, chéri. We would tear the bottom from my ship and I will not permit that to happen. We will wait here for him to sail back out and we will capture him then."

Celeste let out a sigh as if deeply disappointed. In truth, she had ordered her men to find and hunt this dog Bernard when they left the tavern. If all had gone well, one of them should be aboard that vessel. The other... well, time would tell, she hoped.

Jacquotte glanced briefly at her, then ordered one of the pirates to bring up a short stool. "Here," she nudged it with her foot. "Sit and keep watch up here. We'll be preparing the ship." With that, she turned over the glass and nearly flew down the stairs to the deck. Celeste watched her, bemused as she strode the length of the ship, barking orders and gesturing at the rigging and the guns.

Celeste permitted her mind to drift, watching the sea and the rocks for a time, while she dreamt of home. But then she saw the pale outline of a ship's sails against the rock walls. "They're coming!" She called over her shoulder, hoping her voice would carry above the mayhem on the deck, but no further.

Several footsteps raced up the stairs behind her and a large hand plucked the spyglass away. Celeste glared up at a skinny man with a scar running the length of his long face. Jacquotte threw her an amused glance and she staggered to her feet, determined not to be caught off guard.

"Right enough," the fellow grunted as he handed the glass to Jacquotte and gave Celeste an approving nod.

Celeste took a moment to glance at the deck below them and was astonished to discover that the cannon were all hidden below painted clothes. Everything was the color of the deck or of the sea beyond, so the guns might well be invisible from a distance. But why go through so much trouble for one small ship?

She looked up at Jacquotte for answers and noticed that the glass was pointed toward the distant cape now. If she squinted against the sun, she could just make out the sails of several large vessels. "Henry Morgan's ships, awaiting delivery of Fleury's gold." Jacquotte murmured as if she knew Celeste's thoughts. "But we'll hail them first."

The pirate captain bared her teeth in a ferocious grin and Celeste could not suppress a shudder. If the pirates miscalculated, they would be attacked by their quarry and Morgan at the same time. That way lay certain death.

Celeste could not stop herself from glancing away toward the other end of the island. Were there white sails visible in that direction as well? She prayed that it was so. Unless the French ship was in place, she might well have to turn pirate herself.

When she turned back, the rock wall and Bernard's ship were much closer than she expected. There was a brisk exchange in Spanish above her head, the words too fast for her to follow. Then she found herself being towed down to the deck and back to the cabin by the thin man.

"Captain's orders, dulce. No landsmen on deck to get underfoot." He grinned down at her with blackened teeth and gave her an affectionate slap on the buttocks as he crammed her into the cabin where she'd been held earlier. A key turned in the lock as she grabbed for the knob and she cursed Delahaye and her crew heartily.

A few moments later, the ship listed sharply, as if it had struck a rock. Celeste fell to the floor and cursed even harder. She had not thought Delahaye so foolish as to sail too near the shore. From outside, she could hear voices bellowing, then the sound of a ship being hailed. She glanced out the porthole and noted a taut chain that dragged something through the water behind Delahaye's ship.

More shouts from outside, then a moment of silence broken by a barked order. The chain clanked sharply as it was suddenly released. The ship rocked back upright and one cannon, then three suddenly loosed their load. Celeste covered her ears and braced for return fire.

When none came, she reached into her belt and found a thin, narrow piece of metal. She bent it first one way, then the next and inserted it into the lock. She kept trying until the lock turned and she was able to crack the door enough to see out on deck. The other ship was well within range now and it was clear that it had lost sails and part of its mast to the pirates' cannon.

Celeste squinted through the smoke as the ships moved closer. A grappling iron thrown across fell short but she knew it would connect the next time. Smoke was rising from the other ship's hold.

And on the pirate deck, Delahaye was shouting her orders. She carried a pistol in her hand and there was a light in her eyes like that of a woman in love. Celeste looked out to each end of the island, one after the other, checking on Morgan's ships as much as her own. The sails on each were closer now. If they were to take the gold and get away from Morgan, they must do so now.

A hail came from the listing ship. Bernard stood at the prow, hands cupped around his mouth to make his voice carry. Delahaye yelled something back but the wind turned it and shredded it before Celeste could hear it. She suspected that he intended only to buy time until Morgan's ships arrived but it was clear that he would not succeed.

There was a crunch of wood as first one grappling iron, then another found its purchase. Pirates began to wiggle or swing across. A shot from a musket felled one into the water, but then the first of them were over and on the opposite deck. Celeste could hear the clash of blades as she eased her way out of the cabin.

No one seemed to notice as she made her way around the deck. All eyes were trained on their quarry or on Morgan's ships. It was child's play to reach the ropes that bound the ships together, less so to crawl across. As she hung between ships, it gave her a moment's pause to notice that Delahaye's ship was called *The Lioness* while Monsieur Bernard's was *The Antelope*. Had she not been so terrified of falling into the churning waves below, she might have laughed.

As it was, she hung from the swaying rope and hoped that her legs would hold her if her bleeding hands finally released the coarse salt-laden twine. Perhaps she did not need to be a Countess after all. If she disappeared into the jungles of this New World, who would ever know that she had failed in her duty?

Finally, she reached *The Antelope*'s side and managed to ease her trembling body over the rail to collapse on the deck. Once there, she could see that a few of the sailors still fought the pirates. Bernard was in the thick of it, his sword flashing as he repelled as many of Delahaye's crew as he could.

Celeste saw one of the pirates glance her way and turn to alert Jacquotte whose sword even now met Bernard's. She gathered herself for an awkward dash across the smoking deck before diving into the open hold. She landed with a roll that brought her up short against something hard.

She unrolled with a curse and fumbled through the smoke and the darkness for the flint she'd hidden in her leather vest. There must be something down here that she could safely light as a torch. It was then that her nearly deafened ears heard the tell tale crackle of flames coming from somewhere above her. Her heart sank; the French ship would not get here in time. This ship would sink and she would die and vanish along with the gold.

But there was no time to give her fears free rein. The flames would give her a bit of light to see by, as long as she was fast and careful. With a mighty effort, she pulled herself back from the brink of despair and began to look through the objects in the hold. The gold must be here somewhere.

There was a shout from the deck and a figure hurtled down into the hold, landing next to her. She and Monsieur Bernard stared at each other in startled recognition. "You!" He finally hissed. "Louis' little spy! This all your fault!"

"Traitor!" Celeste bellowed.

He swung his sword as she spoke, a great sweep of the blade that might have taken Celeste's head from her shoulders if she hadn't ducked. She felt for her own sword, forgetting that Delahaye's crew had taken it when they kidnapped her.

Bernard's blade passed perilously close to her face and she threw herself backward in an acrobat's roll. When she uncoiled, her hands closed on a loose iron hook, heavy but not so much that she couldn't lift it. Bernard was stumbling toward her now, trying to see in the dim light and the smoke.

She hefted her weapon and swung it, forcing him back for a moment. He brought up his sword and she caught the blade on the hook. For a moment, they wrestled and she held him off. But he was stronger than she was and the blade was coming free.

Using every bit of force she possessed, she kneed him sharply between the legs and he doubled over. But he held onto his blade as she stumbled backward.

"Here." Jacquotte's voice rang out unexpectedly over the noise of the fire. She tossed her cutlass hilt first and Celeste caught it, though barely.

It was nearly as heavy as the hook but she managed to swing it in time to meet Bernard's blade. She could see his face now, teeth set in a snarl as sweat and blood ran down his cheeks. A quick glance upward told her that the flames were spreading: not much time left. She dropped down into a crouch so that he stumbled and shoved him backward while he was still off balance.

Then she swung Jacquotte's sword with all her might, slashing her way across Bernard's belly. He screamed and clutched at himself with his free hand, but still managed to deal Celeste a savage blow with his own blade, cutting her shoulder before she managed to force his blade away. "Slash up! Up!" Jacquotte bellowed from the dimness.

For a moment, Celeste staggered, unable to grasp what the other wanted her to do. Then she turned the blade and sliced Bernard open. He fell with another scream and a liquid thump. Celeste turned away, trying not to be sick. She had never killed like this before.

It almost made her forget the gold. "I'll take that." Jacquotte plucked the blade from her nerveless fingers. "You did well, chéri. Now help me find the gold before this tub sinks."

That brought Celeste back to herself. Moments of frantic searching later Jacquotte stumbled across a locked door in the back of the hold. A single ball from her pistol opened it for them and there they found the chests they sought. Celeste ran a wondering hand through a sea of gold coins, marveling at the wealth before her.

Jacquotte's crew found them then. "Captain!" The mate's eyes were wide. "This tub is spent and both Morgan's men and the *Neptune*, flying the colors of France, are nearly upon us."

Jacquotte stared at Celeste. "Your pistol, Villiers." She took it from his hand and pointed it at Celeste. "Now take two of these chests over to *The Lioness*." Celeste jumped up to protest, but stopped at the look on the pirate's face. "You sent for a ship of your own, mademoiselle. Very clever. Now you shall wait here for them to rescue you."

"You could take me with you. You'll outrun Morgan or maybe even outfight him."

"Best to run. Morgan's ships carry more guns. Now, as regards taking you with me..."

Jacquotte caught her up then, hard arms holding her still while steel fingers trapped her jaw. Then she kissed Celeste, her lips and tongue so surprisingly tender that Celeste found herself surrendering to them.

She wrapped her arms around Jacquotte's neck and kissed her back until it felt as if she might lose herself completely. It was enough to ignore the little voice in her head that screamed that she was committing a mortal sin. What was one more amongst so many? The bearer of the letter had done what she had done.

Celeste gasped as the pirate let her go. "Until next we meet, chéri. Perhaps I will see you at Versailles." Jacquotte moved like a cat, slipping over the side of the wounded ship before Celeste could utter a word. Celeste watched as she swung across on the grappling iron's rope. The pirate ship was cut loose in a span of breaths and began to pull away as the wind filled its sails. Celeste glanced to either side at the ships bearing down on them. Already Morgan's ships were turning to chase the pirates, and Celeste's man had emerged from somewhere to hail *The Neptune*.

Jacquotte stood at the prow of *The Lioness*, Celeste's letter of carte blanche from the King fluttering in her hands. "The bearer of this letter had done what she has done in the service of France," she bellowed over the cheers of her crew. Then she blew Celeste a kiss as the wind caught her ship's sails, leaving Morgan to wallow in its wake.

Celeste pounded her hand on the railing in frustration. When had Jacquotte stolen her letter? And she had only a third of Fleury's gold to show for her efforts. How could she lose so badly? Unconsciously, her fingers touched her lips. She would find a way to recover what was hers; of that, Jacquotte Delahaye might be quite sure.

Great Reckonings, Little Rooms

"...it strikes a man more dead than a great reckoning in a little room."

As You Like It, William Shakespeare

"Let me imagine, since facts are so hard to come, what would have happened had Shakespeare had a wonderfully gifted sister, called Judith, let us say."

A Room of One's Own, Virginia Woolf

Act 1, Scene 1

The young man rubbed the sparse curling hairs on his chin as if their bristles pained him somewhat and sighed as he put his quill back in the ink. The page before him was no less blank than it had been before the sigh so the sound brought him nothing more than the not unwelcome attention of his companion.

She rose from the bed where she reclined and walked toward him, her stride sinuous and seductive under her layers of skirts and bodice. As the light from the window fell on her face, she was not beautiful as beauty is commonly reckoned. No fair English rose here, pale of skin and blonde of hair. Instead she was dark, her complexion the deep olive of the Mediterranean ports, her hair the thick coarse black curls of an Italian peasant. Her lips were full, thick even, and her nose suggested a trace of Jewish blood.

Yet she was beautiful if one had the wit to see it. Her eyes were large and dark and luminous with intelligence, her teeth good and her figure fulsome and promising a glorious bounty to any lover who might strike her fancy. She reached his side before he had time to admire her further and leaned over to wrap her arms around his shoulders.

He closed his eyes and smiled as her lips caressed his neck lightly. His smile widened as her hand slipped down the front of his tunic but he stopped it before it could go further. She pouted at his gesture and snatched a book from the pile on the edge of the table, whirling away laughing.

A step on the stair cut short some of her merriment until a familiar knock sounded at the door. "It's Kit, come to lift your spirits, love!" The dark beauty smiled again as she swept the door open to admit their visitor.

The young man's frown was gone an instant before the man in the doorway might have seen it but somehow, he seemed to know it had been there. Christopher Marlowe swept into the room, a smile that barely reached his eyes twisting his lips. "Not pleased to see me, friend? But then," he caught the volume from the woman's hand, "you're hard at work on your Plautus, I see." He dropped into the chair in front of the table, his sharp gaze missing neither the pile of books or the blank page.

"Come to spy on my progress, eh Kit?" The young man gave his friend a rueful smile that took the edge from his words.

"I had hoped to find you at work on another play. Another play writ anonymously that might catch Henslowe's eye perhaps. Some light fair like your 'Comedy of Errors.' We are all a bit hungrier from the plague." Marlowe's lips twisted in a grimace. "And I myself have little touch for comedy."

"Ah, but your tragedies are for the ages, are they not? And we may all be a bit hungrier but you and Kyd and my brother, you mean. Would that I had the Lord Chamberlain's men speaking my words on stage for a fortnight!" The young man smiled up at the dark temptress at his side and kissed her hand.

The door swung open again, causing them all to start as another young man entered without knocking. This one's countenance was alike to the first's as two peas but for the ferocious scowl he wore and a more fulsome beard. "Hello, Will," murmured the young man at the table.

Kit's smile turned darker, something malicious in it now. "The one and only Shake-scene himself," he murmured.

The scowling man's frown deepened and he responded with a string of oaths that made the playwright laugh. The young woman in contrast, slipped behind the young man's chair. Will gave her a look of pure, frustrated longing before turning his furious glare on the others. "Still playing at being the man, Judith?" He snarled, his gaze locking with that of the seated young man.

The victim of his attack arched an eyebrow and stood with a graceful, catlike stretch. "Would you have me play whore to your poet instead, brother? Or mere muse? These are not roles that I desire."

Once the young man stood, the light caught his face. The contrast picked out the slight delicacy of his features but nothing more suggested femininity. At least not before the other stepped forward so their faces were closer. "Must it be whore then, sister? Surely you might have stayed at home and married a butcher or an innkeeper. Being in foal would look well on you." Will smiled cruelly as the blank page caught his eye. He glanced up to meet

Judith's eyes, knowing how his words would sting, how unlikely it was that any man in Stratford-on-Avon would have her even if she wanted them.

"Careful brother, or you'll turn out to be all that Master Chettle had to say of you, the foul as well as the fair." Judith's lips twisted as her gaze challenged his. How had they come to this, they who had once been as close friends as brother and sister could be? She forced the thought from her face. He must never know how his blows struck home.

Will turned away a moment, shoulders stiff. Then he turned back a breath or two later, stance switching from combatant to orator. Years of acting smoothed away all but the calmest and most pleasant of his expressions. He bowed as if entering the room for the first time, "I shall begin again. Good day, Master Marlowe, Mistress Emilia, sister. I came not to dispense strife, though it comes on my heels, but rather to invite you, one and all to see my poor self appear in a new play of my own devising some days hence."

Kit raised an eyebrow and smiled. "Harlequin and Columbine, perhaps?"

Will gave a genuine laugh, hearty and deep. "It would please you to hear that, wouldn't it, Kit-cat? But no, I must disappoint here as elsewhere." His glance caught Emilia's for a moment. "I am to appear in a fine tragedy, that of *Titus Andronicus*. And it would please me if you were to attend, that afterward we might raise an ale to my new work. That is, if you can do so without being poisoned by jealousy." He favored his sister and Marlowe with an ironic smile.

"I…cannot, Will. But I hope that it may bring you glory." Emilia smiled, only her hands twisting together behind Judith's chair to suggest her agitation. She caught up her cloak and made for the door, but not before Will stepped in front of her and laid his hand on her arm.

"Though your eyes are nothing like the sun, Mistress, yet I would have them look on me kindly. In friendship for better times to come, at least, if the past is not enough." Emilia flinched as Judith surged to her feet and leapt forward only to be stayed by Marlowe's tight grip. Her eyes looked everywhere except at Will for a moment. Then she gave him a tremulous smile and the slightest of nods. A tear shone on her cheek. With a deft twist of her wrist, she broke free and vanished from the room.

Marlowe watched her leave, a strange look crossing his face. He whispered, "Was this the face that launched a thousand ships?" as the door closed but the other two paid no attention to him.

Will stared at the closing door as Judith relaxed in Kit's grip. She spat her words. "Ill done, brother. She loves where her heart goes and you cannot force it elsewhere."

"Put the pretty words to verse, sister and we'll publish it abroad for a shilling or two in my own name. But for now say you will come to my play and see how it is done." He smiled mockingly, then taking their silence for assent, turned on his heel and left without a word of farewell.

Judith slammed her open palm against the chair and bit off an oath before it could leave her lips. Would that she'd been born the man, not Will! The thought rankled her as it had since they were children.

Still, before there was Emilia, Will had been her friend for all that. They had sat together inventing tales and speaking lines for characters of their own invention since Will had taught her to read and write. Each had written poetry of their own but their first plays they had written together. Two minds as one. So of course, when they loved, they must needs love alike.

"I'd say give the girl up, but it's too late for that, isn't it?" Marlowe asked the question in an indifferent tone. He shrugged when she said nothing and gestured at the page. "Can you compose without your brother as muse? Or might another do as well?"

Judith bit her lip and was silent, wondering if Kit was suggesting himself as a replacement. The idea was very nearly too overwhelming to contemplate; the author of *Tamburlaine* offering his patronage to her! Or did he mean something else? No matter, she needed his help, in whatever guise it came. After a long moment, she nodded hesitantly, hoping with all her heart that she did not lie. With that fear uppermost, she pulled a page from beneath the pile of books and handed it to Kit.

He walked under the window and read it, frowning. Then he nodded once and handed it back. "We'll make a writer of you yet, little Jude. Only but finish it, and you'll hear the Chamberlain's Men speak your words as well as any other."

Judith let out a breath she hadn't known she was holding. Marlowe did not give compliments lightly; the work was good. Perhaps she might succeed without Will's help as long as she could play the man.

Kit continued, "Now, I'm off to Deptford to meet with some that I know. A small errand for my other master, the one who is no muse. Come with me and we will raise a mug, there or in better company. You shall be Will as well as any other, at least for today. Nay, better for you are not an angry man in love but a happy lad. Of a sort." Kit smiled, his eyes warming, his charm more than any mortal heart could withstand.

She hesitated, still wondering what Kit really wanted. He kept her secrets and praised her work, even stood her meals from time to time in the months since she had come to London but asked little in return. Perhaps it was nothing more than a desire to be a thorn in Will's side, perhaps only the novelty of tricking the world around them. But if she did not trust him, she had no one else to play the part of brother, not as long as Emilia loved her and not Will. Whatever he wanted from her, she needed him.

Dismissing her misgivings, Judith smiled back as the playacting aspects of such an expedition began to appeal to her. Why should she not be Will for a few hours? She could imitate him so well as to be his shadow; she had done it enough since they were striplings, she should have no trouble doing it now. "Gentle Kit, I would not decline such an invitation were there twenty brothers betwixt us. Let us away to Deptford and the Moor's net." She caught up her belt with its sheathed dagger and fastened it around her doublet. Marlowe bowed, his expression sardonic, as he ushered her out.

Act 1, Scene 2

Lincoln's Inn at Deptford was as like to any other house of its nature as might be: neither fish nor fowl, it was at once neither a public house nor yet merely a home. The innkeeper, one Mrs. Bull, let rooms to some who asked and served ale to many, yet she picked and chose her guests as carefully as she chose her ale and those who drank there often served several masters.

The Queen's spymaster, Sir Francis Walsingham, called "The Moor" for his dark complexion, had known many of the men who drank Mrs. Bull's ale. His ghostly hand lay heavy on the place, for all that he had been dead these three years past. The men who had served him as well as those who came after him worked in both light and shadow, their eyes missing little and their hands at once bloodstained and light-fingered.

This, then was the company that young Judith Shakespeare encountered when she came to Deptford with her friend Kit

Marlowe. But she was not as concerned with the men who watched her as she was with walking as Will would walk, meeting their stares as he would. A sharp-eyed well dressed fellow hailed Kit from a corner table when they entered. "Marcade! Come here!"

'Mercury?' The nickname as well as the command made Judith raise an eyebrow despite her best intentions to keep her features still and impassive. But the fellow was handsome, near blindingly so and Kit had an eye for handsome lads. She stifled a shrug as she trailed after him.

The seated man pulled the playwright down for a hearty kiss on the cheek before his cold, clear gaze fell on her. His expression shifted to something tigerish. "Did you bring your catamite here to parade him before me? Do you plan to govern me through my baser lusts, little Kit-cat?" The words were said softly but with an undertone of menace that sent a chill up her spine.

Kit laughed, the sound cutting through the dark layers in the other's words. He laid a hand on the man's shoulder and grinned back at Judith. "Nay, sweet Tom! I am not such a simpleton as that, though who loves not boys and tobacco is a fool, as I have said before. Yet I know what I have. I give you not my catamite but my rival, Will Shakespeare, whose words are all the talk of London."

"I thought Shakespeare to be older, more manly." The seated man, who Judith realized could be no other than Tom Walsingham, Marlowe's patron and lover and the Moor's own nephew, raked her with a sharp glance. "Not a stripling like this one. He seems as real as your Dutch coin, Kit."

"One man may play many parts on the stage as in the world, my lord," Judith stepped forward with a graceful gesture. "And be as real in one as in any of the others." She gave him one of Will's most charming smiles, the one he wore to calm powerful men who might do him more harm than good.

Walsingham gave her another sharp glance, then nodded. "Well, he has a way with his words, like enough to the one you say he is. Here, make room for my friend Kit and his friend Will." This last command was delivered to the others at the table, one of whom gave Judith an evil look but moved aside nonetheless.

There was something in the fellow's ill-favored countenance, particularly the way he looked at Kit, which had her hand hovering above the dagger on her belt for a breath or two. His pockmarked face nearly burned green in jealous rage whenever Tom looked kindly upon the playwright. She wondered how Kit could bear it.

Yet the moment passed and soon she sat and spoke with Tom and Kit, raising a mug or two of ale until her spirits grew higher than they had in the last fortnight. But Tom's other companions, Poley and Frizer as they were called, cast a pall upon her spirits with their sidelong glances of ill will directed at Kit and soon, at her as well.

Kit plainly thought little of them, the proof in his disdainful manner and after a time, Judith took her cue from him. At first, she mocked them lightly, teasing them about their scowls and their graces. But the atmosphere of ill will did not shift. Finally, the ale loosened her tongue more than she had intended and she met Frizer's eyes with a fierce glare of her own. "Fellow, your looks are foul enough to sour good ale. Your manners mark you as churlish a cur as I have ever met. Have you fair wit or words to balance them?"

Tom laughed and Kit's lips curled in an amused grimace, though his frown sent her a quick warning. By then, it was too late. Frizer lurched to his feet, hand on his knife, and Poley caught his arm. He shook Poley off as he hissed, "Codpiece sniffing sodomite! Are you a heretic as well?" He jerked his chin at Kit. "Don't be in such a hurry to welcome your master below." With that, he turned on his heel and left.

This time it was Kit who laughed. "Am I heretic now? Such is the price of loyal service!" He glanced at Tom, his expression angry and wary all at once yet Tom was silent. His expression told Judith nothing but Kit must have found some comfort in his face because his posture relaxed somewhat.

Poley stood and announced that he must leave for other errands. He slipped away so quietly the others scarcely noticed his departure. Judith gave Kit a worried frown. A charge of sodomy was ill enough; to add heresy to it meant a trip to the executioner's block if it were proven. Or if you had no protection. She wondered if Tom would stand by him if the worst happened.

But no more was said. They drank more ale, debating the best of the new plays until Kit and Tom began to discuss philosophy and Judith fell silent. Her education had been slipshod, gleaned from the pickings of her brother's learning since their father saw no need for a girl to know such things. Still, it was fascinating and she absorbed all she could, Frizer and Poley forgotten in the flow of words until it was time for them to return to their rooms.

Act 2, Scene 1

Judith didn't see the bill posted on the church wall until three days after her night in Deptford. She was coming from the printer's office where she had pled her case for the publishing of a new play, not yet finished, when it caught her eye. The first few lines were a spiteful piece of venom accusing the Dutch of treachery and cowardice in their war with Spain, causing brave English soldiers to die in their stead. She might have ignored it but for the signature: Tamburlaine.

That was enough to make her stop and read it through. The play had been Kit's masterwork, the one that her brother and Kyd and all the other playwrights sought to emulate. It could be no accident that the name appeared on this document.

But had Kit written it himself? She scanned the verses; they seemed too clumsy for his hand, despite the touches that suggested his skill. And what had he to do with the Dutch? There was no connection as far as she knew, save what Tom had said of "Dutch coin." But she could make no sense of that so perhaps it was nothing, the words some private jest between the two. She turned away, trying to convince herself of that.

The words nagged at her though, filling her thoughts until she found herself at Kit's rooms some hours later. He should know of this, even if it had naught to do with him. At least he might be on his guard if something more lay beyond the verses than simple malice.

But he was not to be found at his room and the landlord sent her on to Tom Walsingham's lodgings. They too were deserted. A servant there said that his master had gone to the country and that Master Marlowe might have gone with him. He would say no more and Judith had no coin with which to press her case. She turned reluctantly from the house and walked home.

Emilia was waiting for her there, having stolen a few hours from her husband's side. She forgot the poem and Kit and even her brother in her lover's body.

The next few days passed quickly. She wrote and read what she had written to Emilia. She saw Will's new play and found the words to praise it. He glowed a bit, almost as he had before Emilia came between them. She wondered if he would find that glow of goodwill sufficient to read her new play, but she decided to wait. She would show it to Kit first. Whenever he reappeared.

Act 2, Scene 2

When two more days passed without word, she could stand it no longer. She left her room that afternoon to walk to Deptford. It took some time to make the journey, which gave her ample time for thought.

She could not have said why she went now, except that there were rumors about the flyers that she'd seen, rumors that mentioned Kit. And Thomas Kyd had been arrested and charged with heresy, or so the whispers said. True, Kyd was no friend of hers and she liked his stiff prose little enough. But he was a friend of Kit's and if the charge fell on one, it might well fall on another. The thought chilled her

For this expedition, she had added more hair to her chin with an actor's art, forcing her face into a near mirror of Will's. It might give her extra protection on the street or in the inn if she appeared older, fiercer. She remembered Frizer's rage and shivered with no ale to warm her against it. Still, she must know what had happened to Kit; surely he could not have moved permanently to the country. It would prove too dull for such as he.

The inn was where she remembered it and the men at the tables were much the same. But this time she entered cautiously, searching for Mrs. Bull and whatever information she could provide and meeting few men's eyes. The common room was near to empty in any case so there were few enough to see her. She crept to the kitchen, then waited while the kitchen boy fetched the landlady.

When she finally appeared, her sharp black eyes studied Judith as if she was some new specimen, an exotic creature wafted in from far off lands. Judith stammered her questions and Mrs. Bull merely looked at her for a few moments. When at last she spoke, her voice was thick with unvoiced amusement. "One of Master Marlowe's friends, are you? Odd that he'd not have told you where he might be going if he was leaving London."

That lent steel to Judith's backbone. "I'm merely here to deliver a message and his landlord said I might find him here. It's all the same to me whether he drinks your ale or another's." She drew herself up and gave the other woman her haughtiest look.

Mrs. Bull made a dry sound like bones rattling that might have been a chuckle. "I'll not be telling tales of Master Marlowe but if he's to come here, it will be with Master Walsingham after sunset. Spend your coin here or elsewhere until then." The innkeeper shrugged and turned back to the kitchen, leaving Judith in the doorway.

She accepted her dismissal reluctantly, turning away to peer out the window at the murky sky outside. It was hard to tell when darkness would fall but it could not much longer, surely. She groped in her pouch for coin and found a scant few shillings. Just enough to buy her ale and a bowl of stew, even here.

Taking a deep breath, Judith slipped onto an empty bench in a dark corner and beckoned a servant. Food and drink arrived soon after and Judith bent her head to the task of eating, only looking up when the door swung open for those entering and leaving. It seemed like an eternity though the food was good. Men came and went but none were Kit or Walsingham.

At last she was done eating and drinking and had no more coin to allow her to linger. She stood slowly and made her way to the door in time for it to swing open, leaving her face to face with Frizer. He recognized her instantly, despite the extra beard she had carefully applied. The scent of beer hung over him like a cloud. "It's another sodomite heretic! 'Tis our lucky day, Poley. The Privy Council will pay well for this one too, I think." He herded Judith back into the room with an evil smile.

Poley and another man followed at his heels, the former giving her a glance of pure contempt. There would be little help from that quarter, she realized. Her brain spun with ideas for escape at the same time that she wrestled with his words. The Privy Council? Was Kit in the Tower?

Frizer's grip on her shoulder tightened, driving her fears for Kit from her head for the moment. He fumbled for the knife at his belt, eyes glowing with drunken bloodlust. She summoned anger as a shield. "Devil take thee, cur! What do you mean by laying your hands on me?" She twisted sharply and jumped back a pace or two, causing her assailant to stumble into the room, releasing her. Her hand was on her own knife but she didn't unsheathe it yet. There might yet be time to end this with words, before her clumsiness with a blade was revealed.

Frizer's unknown companion caught him as he staggered sideways and shoved him toward a table. Poley stepped close to Judith, overwhelming her with the stale scent of his breath. "Begone, little whoreson. Your protector is going to burn and Ingram here will sink his knife in your belly if you stay. And that would be a waste of good steel." He tossed her roughly toward the door as Frizer lurched to his feet, bellowing.

Judith fled, raucous laughter pursuing her onto the streets of Deptford. She ran as if pursued by demons, fleet-footed and unassailed for the safety of her room. When she reached it, she slammed the door behind her, her heart racing as she gasped for air and locked the night out. She berated herself for cowardice until she could stay awake no longer. Then she collapsed on the bed, falling eventually into a night of ill dreams, haunted by fearful visions of Kit on the block and her own shamefaced return to her father's home in Stratford or worse.

Act 3, Scene 1

The next two nights she passed playing a lad in one of the plays that Lord Strange's company was staging. There was still no word from Kit and she began to fear that he was already dead.

On the third day, Will came to see her just before she left for the theater. "I bring you joy of the play, sister. You are as fine a lad as ever tread the boards, myself excepted." He bowed with a flourish and Judith laughed despite her worries.

"Thank you for your kindness, brother. You have been many a fine lad so this is praise indeed. On another point before I must leave, have you had word of Kit?"

Will gave her an impish grin and flourished a grubby bit of paper at her. "Not from Kit but from one close to him."

She took the note, reading and rereading it in increasing bewilderment. "What does this mean?"

Will snorted at her slow wit. "It is an invitation to dine with a powerful man whose patronage can only advance my plays. Surely your foolish jealousy cannot blind you to the advantages of such a relationship?"

"But Will, Tom is Kit's patron and--"

"Perhaps he seeks a better playwright. No, say no more, little sister. I understand that you would stand a friend to Kit but I cannot, nay will not decline such an opportunity."

Judith remembered Tom's cold face when the words "sodomite" and "heretic" were spoken and shivered. He would let Kit go the block or the flames and acquire a new protégé. Still she tried what she could to dissuade Will, but it was no use and she had to leave for the theater. When she returned, she longed for Emilia to come but her beloved remained as absent as Kit. She passed another restless night in frightening dreams, filled with the premonition of ills to come.

The next morning, Judith was awakened by a familiar knock at the door shortly after dawn. Heart pounding, she rose, tugging on a doublet and picking up her knife as she moved to stand by the door. Hand on the heavy oak, she asked, "Kit?"

"Open the door, little one. I'm here alone." Kit's voice, certainly but in a voice that sounded too feeble to be his own.

Judith hesitated a moment, then unbarred the door. Kit stood on the other side, covered in blood, his eyes red and his hands trembling. She recoiled backward, giving him room to enter.

He lurched inside, sinking onto the bed with a quiet groan. Now that he was out of the darkened hall, she could see the marks of torture on him: bruises and cuts too systematic to be natural. It wrung her heart and she fetched a pitcher of water to wash him clean. He said nothing while she ministered to his wounds, only the hiss of his breath to tell her when something hurt more that it should.

At last, she held a mug of flat beer to his lips and let him lie back on her bed. He closed his eyes and his body went slowly limp as he fell asleep. She looked down at him, frowning for a long moment. But it seemed cruel to wake him merely to satisfy her curiosity; any danger he brought to her door might have found her by other means anyway.

Instead she barred the door again then moved to her chair and table, taking up her quill as she gnawed on a piece of bread. She had been thinking of a play that revolved around twin brothers, not unlike Will and her. The point scratched busily on the page before her as the plot took shape.

Act 3, Scene 2

She had written a nearly an entire act when Kit finally sat up with a groan and dropped his head into his hands. Judith stood and stretched, her back and hands stiff from her labors, before she spoke. "What happened, Kit? I looked for you everywhere, even in Deptford."

Kit looked up, eyes sharp in his alarmed face. "You went back there looking for me? Did anyone see you?"

Judith shuddered at the memory of Frizer's furious eyes. "That cur who drank with us when we went there, Frizer. And Poley. Frizer tried to draw his blade on me but was too far in his cups. I ran…ran as fast as I could from the place." She hung her head, cheeks burning under her beard. A real man would have stayed to fight. She waited for Marlowe's scorn.

Kit swore, a string of colorful oaths falling from his cut lips. Then he laughed quietly. "They say that he stumbles who runs fastest, yet I'm glad to hear that you eluded the blade so that you might stand friend to me today. As to Frizer, he is a dangerous dog. I advise you to run swiftly away again whenever you may see him next." He closed his eyes again.

"Were you in the Tower, Kit? I heard tales of the Privy Council, of charges of heresy." Judith waited but Kit was silent, his face turned toward the floor. When she could stand it no longer, she spoke again. "Will told me yesterday that he intended to steal your patron Walsingham away but since you are here and free, I can see that this is not so." She attempted to laugh lightly but the sound died away when she saw Kit's face. "What is it?"

Kit stood, swaying a little and walked to her table, murmuring softly, "What further mischief is this? What did he say?" He frowned, his face flushing until Judith was well and truly frightened.

"It was an invitation to dine with…Tom Walsingham in Deptford. But the note did not seem as if he had written such a thing. I tried to persuade Will but he would hear nothing of it. Is

Will in some danger, Kit?" She caught his sleeve. "Is it the Privy Council or something else?"

Kit's eyes were wild and he pulled a scrap of a note from his doublet. "A note like this one?

Judith stared and nodded. "Whence came this to you, Kit?"

"My jailor gave it to me as he opened the door of my cell. I think we must go and find Will. I do not like this, little Jude; it is not Tom's way to commit more to the page than he must." He paused, seeming to gather his thoughts, "But first, we must disguise me. My looks are not popular on the streets today. Have you still your skirts and maiden's garb?"

Act 3, Scene 3

It was but the work of a short hour to make Kit into a plain but believable maid. Judith laughed a bit to see him in her old gown and even he began to smile a bit at last. When all was complete, they left to go in search of Will.

But he was not to be found at any of his usual haunts and Judith was struck with a terrible fear. She ached inside, empty of the weight of her brother in her heart for the first time in many years. Kit stumbled at her side, cutting into her thoughts, and she reached out to steady him as if he were a maid in truth. He was exhausted, the dark circles under his eyes making them glitter feverishly in contrast to his white face.

She caught his arm and turned them to walk back to her room just as a coach rattled across the street before them and stopped. Tom Walsingham's sharp-featured face met her gaze impassively from the interior before he swung the door open without a word.

Judith looked to Kit for guidance but found none. He was spent, his complexion grey with pain and effort. She wrapped her arm around his waist and hauled him forward, pulling him into the coach with Tom's help. She followed and Tom signaled to the driver to start up again. He studied Kit in his skirts for a long moment, lips curled in an odd smile. But his expression still held a ghost of tenderness, which helped to reassure her; he might save Kit yet.

Finally he turned to her. "I am astonished to find you here, Master Shakespeare. I had had other news of you that suggested I might not find you in this life again." Judith stiffened but he continued before she could say anything else. "I am glad to see that it is otherwise with you."

"What is it you know, my lord? Do you have some word of my broth…" She caught herself a moment too late.

"A brother? Faith! That would explain it then. I fear I have ill news for you, Master Shakespeare but let us only reach the inn and see what is to be done before we speak more."

Judith stared at him, her mind awhirl with horror and misgiving. Then Kit moaned as the wheels hit a hole and they both turned to him, Tom pulling his cape from his shoulders and tucking it around him. "Poor boy. I would that I could have taken this hurt from you," he murmured. He pulled Kit's head to his shoulder but would say no more until the coach began to lurch its way into Deptford.

The Lincoln Inn looked much the way it had when Judith had fled it last. This time however, Frizer and Poley emerged to meet the coach. Frizer's eyes shifted guiltily under Walsingham's hard stare and he stammered his words a bit. "We thought it a game, my lord. We thought that to teach the young gamecock a lesson while we carried out your other orders…my lord, he drew his blade first. We wrestled for it--" He stopped as Judith threw herself out of the coach, his jaw agape as if he was seeing a ghost.

She shoved her way past him and dashed into the inn. Mrs. Bull caught her eye and pointed silently upstairs. She reached the landing as if she had wings. There she tried each door until she found the one she sought. Tom and Kit followed on her heels until all three stood over a corpse that might have been Judith's own, but for some thickness of the frame, some weight about the jaws.

Judith dropped to her knees, sobbing hysterically and Tom closed the door as she wailed, "It was meant to be me. I insulted them, me, not Will!"

"And I believe that it was actually meant to be me, was it not, sweet Tom?" Kit's voice was like cold water on her grief and she sat up, tears still pouring down her face. "You feared that I might speak under the Council's caresses and betray you, did you not? Your curs without were to lure me here and slay me alone but they thought to rid themselves of another annoyance as well. Is it not so, sweet Tom?"

Kit and Tom faced each other over Will's bloody body, staring at each other as if there was no corpse between them. Kit's face was nearly as pale as Will's but his eyes were steady. In the end, it was Tom who dropped his gaze first. "I cannot stand against a heresy charge, Marcade. Not that and…the other. I would be sent to the block."

"And if it twere merely my own life?" Kit spoke swiftly, his pain touching each word.

Tom flinched, looking at Judith for the first time since he entered. "Know that I am sorry. He was never meant to die." Judith glared back at him, shaking with fury and reaction. "Still," he continued as if there was nothing more to be said, "this may yet be put to good account."

"I have lost my truest friend!" Judith shouted, lurching to her feet, right hand fumbling for the hilt of her blade. Kit stepped between her and Tom, placing his hands on her shoulders. She struggled with him a moment and he pressed her to him in a tight embrace, holding her until she went limp, body shuddering.

Then Kit turned back to Tom. "You have killed me as well as Will. I cannot stay here with a price on my head. England's theaters may never recover from it. What good account can you make of slaying the future?"

Tom frowned. "Hear my thoughts, gentle sirs. Kit must die, either here or on the block. The Queen's justice demands his blood for his crimes against God and nature. Therefore, Christopher known as Marlowe dies here this day in Deptford." He gestured at Will's body. "The plays may be written in France or Italy as well as here. Will yet stands before us and if he has his brother's way with words, he can be your voice in England, Marcade."

Judith slumped against Kit's shoulder, knowing it was the only way to save him. Then it was left only for coin to cross a few palms, enough to say that one Christopher Marlowe, atheist and blaspheming heretic, poet and playwright, had died that day. The witnesses were called, their testimony taken. And by then, Judith and Kit had been dismissed, sent home where her despair would not confuse the telling of the tale.

Act 4, Scene 1

Kit stood staring out the window, a small sack of his goods packed for a journey at his feet. "Well, little Judith, it seems there are just two of us left now to make one good playwright." He said at last. "And I think I must call you Will to grow accustomed to the name in my mouth." He stared out onto the surrounding roofs for a long moment before he turned back to face her.

She sniffled once or twice more, then rubbed her face with the back of her hand. She found her voice with an effort. "But I have no gift for tragedy."

"Nor I for comedy."

"And the sonnets? What of those?"

Kit reached over and caught up a page from the pile on the table. He studied it a moment and his lips quirked in a wry smile. "I think that together we might manage. The new play?" He reached out a hand to accept the handful of pages she held out.

"But what of your own plays, your own poems, Kit?"

"I am dead, little Will who was Judith. What use have dead men for such things?"

"I can sell them for you. Only give me a letter dated before this week, saying that you left them to me. I will deliver them for you and send you the coin." Judith spoke eagerly. "Think of how they will fight to publish them now that you are…dead." She faltered over the word.

Kit nodded as the idea took root. "And I will send you new tragedies from France, Italy, Spain and whatever other Popish hells I may visit ere I can return to England once more." He looked away from her to the pages in his hands. Like quicksilver, he flipped through them, even laughing aloud once or twice. "Twins, mistaken identities and the lovers reunited at the end of it all. You are in truth the one and only comic Shakespeare." He gave her a deep bow.

Judith shook her head, taking the pages back. "Merely half, Kit. And never quite whole again, I think." She wiped her cheek again, picked up her quill and began to write.

Regency Masquerade

"Bath!" shrieked the Misses de Clercy in unison, in much the same way they did everything else. Or so it sometimes seemed to their cousin, Isabella as she gazed down at her fancy work and sternly reminded herself not to look across the room.

There the two Misses, Clara and Emily, sat in all their golden blue-eyed beauty on either side of their mother. She was a stout lady of middle years, quite as pink with enthusiasm as her daughters. The sight (and she saw it often) always had the same effect as a surfeit of sweets. Perhaps it was only that they all favored gowns of pale blue muslin with pink ribbons that made them all so charmingly similar. She sighed at the thought, only to become increasingly aware that six twinkling blue eyes were fixed upon her, awaiting her response.

"Bath," she echoed, with considerably less enthusiasm. A vision of interminable balls where her card was filled by second sons all eager to cavort upon her dainty feet hovered before her eyes. There would be (here, she shuddered delicately) *officers*.

She made a small grimace of disgust and could almost feel the headache coming on. The cheerful exhortations of Mrs. de Clercy to dance with just one more eligible young man would mingle mercilessly with the drone of an overly ambitious string quartet, and she would end as unwed as she began. In short, it would be like last Season.

The thought was more than she could bear. The Forsythes were still looking for a governess to take charge of their little horrors. Perhaps this year, even kindly Mrs. de Clercy could be persuaded that no one, not even a dragoon, would have the hand of a nearly penniless orphan. No more than she would have them. Her elegant dark head tilted proudly. She could make her own way in the world.

Clara de Clercy chose that moment to leap to her feet and seize Isabella's hands, tugging her from both her thoughts and her seat in a single impetuous motion. She spun her cousin in a quick circle, fancywork flying away as Isabella was forcibly reminded that her cousins were not so alike as she occasionally thought them.

Laughing, Clara then caught up her younger sister's hand and together they whirled Isabella from the room in a torrent of laughter and trailing pink ribbons. Mrs. de Clercy's plaintive, "Don't jump so, girls. T'isn't proper," followed them up the stairs. There Isabella's resistance soon proved futile and she found herself donning her best green wool walking dress. After that it was the work of moments to find herself, cousins in tow, walking at a brisk pace to the dressmaker's shop in the nearby village of Pickled Alderberry.

Preparations for removal to Bath filled the following days. Clara and Emily's kindly attentions to Isabella's wardrobe left her with little opportunity to think of anything else. She surrendered to this flood of enthusiasm with only a slight twinge of guilt about the expense. Perhaps this Season would be different, she thought hopefully. If not, the Forsythes would have probably gone through at least two governesses by end of the year and would be in need of a third.

In truth, as she sat in the pleasant parlor neglecting the novel before her, she had to admit that she didn't really want to go into service. Unfortunately, it often seemed her only prospect, penniless as she was, despite her fine style and the green eyes which had smitten several admirers. Such was not the future that even her somewhat irregular parents had envisioned for her, though she was unclear as to what her mother, the authoress, and her father, the philosopher, had contemplated for their only child.

Their untimely passing in the summer fever epidemic two years before had settled the issue and their daughter in to the hands of their amiable and conventional cousins, the de Clercys. Isabella sighed and wiped away a tear at the memory, causing Clara to cross the room to embrace her, smashing several pages of the book as she did so.

Certainly Isabella could not have asked for more kindly relations. She reflected upon this with great frequency two days later, as their post chaise ambled toward the great metropolis some fifty miles away while the Misses exclaimed gleefully at each new sight, and even some old ones.

"Look! A barouche!" commented Emily for the third time that day as one passed their coach. How fortunate, Isabella thought, as she stared out the window, that now there was nothing else to see except the deserted road and some gloomy woods running alongside it.

"Isn't it just like Mrs. Radcliffe?" Clara exclaimed. She had but recently finished that famous novelist's splendid *Udolpho* and could, perhaps, be forgiven for her enthusiasm.

At that, Mrs. de Clercy awakened sufficiently to respond to this flight of fancy, "Nonsense, dear! Wherever would we find Italian banditti on the road to Bath!" Having delivered this bit of maternal wisdom, she returned placidly to her nap.

Still, as Clara pointed out, the moment her mama's mouth dropped open in a gentle wheeze, since Mr. de Clercy had gone on ahead to attend to business, they were in fact three lovely young maidens traveling virtually unprotected on a deserted road. "It is very like *Udolpho*," she insisted, cheerfully ignoring the presence of the armed outrider who rode behind the chaise.

It was at that moment that the carriage lurched to a halt and there was a shout from the box. A shot rang out and a deep voice bellowed "Stand and deliver!"

Mrs. de Clercy, jolted suddenly awake, gasped, "What is it?"

"I believe," said Isabella, her calm tones belying her racing heart, "that we are being held up." She gingerly withdrew the pistol from its holster in the door and slipped it beneath a fold of her skirt in case it should be needed. She endeavored, as she did so, to conceal it from her companions. There was no necessity at present for causing needless alarm. Or "alarum" as some of the novels would have it. She found she could not suppress the thought, despite the gravity of the situation.

A pair of gleaming dark eyes in a masked face appeared at the window. Below them there was a rather slender hand attached to a solid looking pistol. This sight quickly restored her to decorum. As the bandit opened the door and gestured them out of the coach, Isabella contrived to keep her pistol hidden. She studied the slender robber with great interest, having never seen one outside of a book before. In contrast, he ignored them in favor of searching their possessions.

His compatriot, a burly man also disguised by a mask, held a brace of pistols on the coachman, the postillions and the disarmed outrider. Seeing this, Isabella determined not to display her pistol unless absolutely necessary, for it would not do to cause one of the party to be murdered for something as paltry as their jewelry.

She was pleased to find that though she had, in point of fact, never shot anything but a target, she was prepared to take whatever action became necessary. The realization lent steel to her backbone and she drew herself up, appearing even taller and more elegant than she ordinarily did.

As she continued to study the slim rogue who seemed to be the leader, it struck her that there was something vaguely familiar about him, though she could not imagine what it was. Even her parents didn't consort with highwaymen. So fixed were her thoughts that she jumped when he broke the silence by demanding in a hoarse voice that they place their money and jewelry into his hat, which he held out for that purpose.

He walked down the line of quaking de Clercys, giving each a polite bow as she complied with his demands until he reached Isabella. Looking up slightly to meet her eyes he seemed almost to start as though seeing her for the first time. He paused a long moment. "From you, my fine lady, I want only a kiss," he growled, eyes flashing with an unreadable gleam from behind the black mask.

This was beyond enough. Isabella raised the pistol to the level of his heart. "I hardly think so," she responded, far more calmly than she felt at that moment. "I am a fair shot and I do not think I would be likely to miss at this range." Mrs. de Clercy, who had been of increasingly ashen hue, chose that moment to faint.

The rogue looked around, and seeing that Clara and Emily had gone to their mother's assistance and that the men on the box had his companion to occupy them, glanced back at Isabella and whispered, "Not even for me, Belle?"

Isabella froze. That voice. She knew it, somehow. Her hand drooped, tilting the pistol downward, just long enough for her unoccupied hand to be pressed ardently to soft lips before the highwayman was onto his horse and away. He and his compatriot soon vanished down the road.

Isabella remained outwardly cool and soon had Mrs. de Clercy restored to rights through judicious use of smelling salts. The party was on the road again, though they went only as far as the next inn. There they immediately stopped for the night, being far too flustered to continue on until morning.

Indeed, though not overly flustered herself, Isabella had much to think about as she lay staring at the broad beamed ceiling of the room that she shared with Clara. First, of course, there was her gratitude to the memory of her dear departed father who taught her to shoot.

But of far more importance to her sleepless mind were the actions of the rogue who took the de Clercy's jewelry. Why should his voice sound familiar? Why would such a scoundrel know her childhood name and demand a kiss from her? Why, it was, to her credit she felt, that the only lips which had ever touched hers were those of her particular friend, Olivia Sandleford. Dear Olivia, her dearest, and indeed, her only friend at Miss Havershere's School for Young Ladies, had vanished into the jungles of Brazil with her family some four years before.

Isabella never thought upon her without a tear rolling down her lovely cheek. Her time with Olivia had been the most pleasant period of her education, particularly those times when their lips met in chaste and lively affection. Miss Havershere viewed it differently, of course, but she was a vulgar person, incapable of seeing the manner in which true friendship transcended such nonsensical restraints as a rather stiff propriety.

In truth, Isabella remembered that neither Olivia's family or her own saw fit to reprimand them for their behavior. The goat that they placed in Miss Havershere's bed, on the other hand, did result in their expulsion from their little grotto of scholarship. Then there was scarcely time for prolonged farewells before Olivia and the Sandlefords vanished with the rest of the ambassadorial staff to the other side of the world. Olivia's last letter arrived some months after, with the lines so crossed over each other that Isabella could barely read it. She had declared her undying love and friendship, then was never heard from again.

Isabella sighed at the memory, then paused. Why was she thinking now about Olivia? There had been something about that highwayman...Had Olivia a brother? She vaguely recalled that there had indeed been such a person, though she had never met him. The look in the eyes, the use of her childhood name, the voice...Isabella's green gaze narrowed in a look that did not bode well for someone.

How did Olivia's brother (she suddenly felt quite certain the robber must be he) come to act the highwayman on a road to Bath? Why did he seem to know her when he had never seen her before? She resolved to say nothing to the de Clercys until she got to the bottom of this. When she did, one young gentleman of a good family was going to deeply regret his actions. She drifted off into satisfying dreams about having him tarred and feathered.

He filled her thoughts the next morning as well. Perhaps he had done it on a wager? It was an understandable, if contemptible motivation. Young men often fell prey to such notions if encouraged by foolish friends. Or so she had heard.

Isabella pondered this and other possibilities as her party was handed into the coach, surrounded now by three outriders armed to the very teeth. Their journey resumed without further incident, giving her ample time for her ruminations until they reached their destination.

Mr. de Clercy, a sturdy gentleman who in both girth and years somewhat exceeded his good wife, met them at a respectable town house in Laura Place. It was not far from the Pump Room and thus promised to be a most suitable residence for the Season.

His beloved helpmeet and daughters lost no time in telling him of the terrors of the ride. "Good heavens! Highwaymen on the road to Bath! This must be brought to the attention of the authorities!" His very side whiskers bristled in indignation. No sooner were they settled, in body, if not in spirit, then he was off to the local magistrate's home to demand prompt and immediate action.

At that moment Isabella belatedly remembered that the penalty for robbery on the King's highways was the end of a rope. Plainly, her beloved friend's brother (she found that she could think of him in no other light) must be stopped before such a precipitous end. But how to even find him, let along stop him?

That question occupied her mind quite fully through teatime and beyond into the next day until her relations thought she was quite undone by her courage on the road. The incident had left Clara and Emily much in awe of their cousin, but now seeing her so withdrawn, they became concerned for her health. In Bath, there could be one answer for that: first a visit to the Pump Room then dancing at the Assembly Rooms, and so they promptly embarked upon a cure.

The Season was far enough advanced that the Pump Room was pleasantly full of families acquainted with the de Clercys, all concerned with taking the waters and greeting each other. But as her cousins were not so preoccupied so as to forget their fair cousin, Isabella found both Mrs. de Clercy and Emily each presenting her with a glass of the celebrated waters.

"You must drink, dear Isabella. It was so restorative when Mama felt faint last year. Do you not remember?" Emily gazed earnestly up at her older cousin.

"The waters will restore your nerves in no time, love. Even after such a shock as the one that we had," Mrs. de Clercy suited her actions to her words and sipped urgently upon her own glass, gloved hand trembling ever so slightly.

Isabella responded with a grateful smile, though in truth the scent of the waters was quite as restorative as she thought she could endure without the additional pain of actually drinking them. She sipped slowly until her party's attentions turned elsewhere, then surreptitiously poured both glasses out.

Now freed from her burden, she could examine the room at her leisure. There was, indeed, much to be seen.

Across the room a very Pink of the Ton with his collar so stiff and high that the points nearly blinded him, raised his monocle to study the Misses de Clercy from his corner. His coat of blue superfine was cinched in tight at the waist, causing it to nearly rival those of well born ladies of a century before. The shining threads of a truly perilous waistcoat gleamed in the light of the window by which he stood. His dark brown locks were curled *a la Corsair* in the manner of the disreputable Byron and so full and intricate was the tying of his cravat that it must have taken his valet hours before he was fit to leave the house.

Yet for all that, Isabella conceded that he would have been quite handsome in a very delicate way were he not such a popinjay. He, too, seemed familiar to her, resembling Olivia in coloring, though not of course in sex. At that moment, she began to fear for her mind. Must everyone she encountered seem not only familiar to her but reminiscent of her lost friend? This must stop, she remonstrated with herself.

She soon found that she had gone on studying the unknown gentleman past the bounds of propriety. He must have felt her eyes upon him for his scrutiny turned next to her, causing her to blush, which she hated. He favored her with a very stiff bow, which she disliked even more. Then he turned to examine a newly arrived party who all seemed to claim his acquaintance.

She looked swiftly and guiltily away, only to have her gaze pulled back by their cry of greeting.

"Freddie Sandleford! Upon my word, I had not thought to find you so far from London during the Season, sir!" A hearty young gentleman, clad in a well used hunting jacket, trotted forward to wring his hand, the two young ladies of his party scarcely a step behind.

Isabella looked sharply back at the gentleman. That had been the name of Olivia's brother, but *this* simply couldn't be the same man who had robbed them. His bearing was so different; true, they were of a size and he had dark eyes like Olivia herself, but the expression! So cool and proud! Clearly this was not a man who disguised himself as a highway bandit, Isabella told herself quite sternly.

Clara and Emily chose that same moment to approach her and she turned away determined to look no more. Still, some moments later, as they gathered at the door to return to Laura Place to prepare for the Assembly Rooms, Isabella could not help feeling his eyes upon her. She glanced over at him again and found him studying her, quite as she had examined him earlier. A smile softened the thin lips (so very like Olivia's!) and gave his eyes an almost wistful look as he bowed again, but here she knew herself to be misguided.

Certainly, she was not out of the common way, though her friends had tried to tell her otherwise in terms that she knew to be nothing but well meant flattery. Why, her cousins both outshone her in their pink and gold beauty, and few young gentlemen would gaze longingly at her as she stood beside them. She dropped her eyes and turned resolutely away.

It was soon discovered that this exchange had not gone as unnoticed as she would have preferred. "He's very handsome," Clara offered as she tucked an arm through her cousin's. "We must know someone who could produce an introduction." She smiled merrily up at her cousin, who had the grace to blush for the second time that day.

"I merely thought that I recognized the gentleman. I was mistaken. Such style and address are far above my station, of course: he must be at least a baronet," she offered in tones so rich in irony that Clara burst into peels of laughter.

"Oh Isabella, you are too bad! True, he does not look clever enough by a half for you! And that waistcoat! Oh!" Clara was greatly amused. Her shoulders shook with mirth.

Isabella felt, a bit resentfully, that Clara was far too much at ease for her first Season but there was no help for it. Under other circumstances she would have been merely amused, but it would not do to have Clara's romantic notions suggesting a *tendre* where none existed. She took some care to turn the conversation into other waters.

The rest of the rather long afternoon was spent preparing for their grand entrance to the Assembly Rooms. Isabella's tedium was broken only by the mildly shocking news that tonight's ball was to be masked for the first few hours, with masks to be removed at ten o'clock. Only the sanction of the redoubtable and respectable Lady Peavsey sufficed for Mr. de Clercy to permit them to attend such an event, however reluctantly.

One pleasant thought had occurred to Isabella: perhaps the Tulip from the Pump Room was indeed Olivia's brother, and not the highwayman at all. Then, if she could contrive an introduction, he could tell her whether she lived and where she was. The thought brought color to her cheeks and animation to her eyes as she was fastened into her new gown.

"Oh, you look splendid! Do not these colors suit us all admirably? We will dance every dance tonight!" Clara declared, eyes aglow, turning from side to side in front of the mirror until her somewhat forgivable enthusiasm infected her sister. It was, after all, their first real Season.

Isabella sank back into quietly languorous misery and wondered if dance shoes could be made which actually protected the feet from the onslaught of the enthusiastically clumsy. Still, despite her misgivings, the three were all finally ready for their entrance to the Rooms to the great joy of Sophie, their maid.

After hours of preparation, it was with a joyous heart and tired feet that the good woman watched her handiwork move down the stairs. They looked well enough that every dance card should be filled, giving her plenty of time for a good soak before they returned, she thought with some measure of glee.

Isabella, elegant though she was in her new muslin gown of apple green adorned with dark green ribbons and a pretty black velvet domino, envied Sophie her soak more than anyone could have imagined. She passed the journey trying mightily to forget the trials of the last Season.

When they arrived at their destination, the crush of carriages before the Rooms was such that they chose to get out and walk the remaining distance to the doors. Isabella, walking apprehensively at Mrs. de Clercy's side, could not repress a thought: Oh, if only Olivia were here by her side! Together they could have made light of all of this nonsense. She lapsed into a distracted vision of seeing Olivia again that quite blinded her to the blaze of candlelight and the overpowering noise of polite conversation that greeted their entrance.

Once inside, Mrs. de Clercy's efforts on her charges' behalf proved successful. Lady Peavsey was quite pleased to introduce several eligible young gentlemen to their party, leaving Mrs. de Clercy to happily take her seat with the other mamas and chaperones as the cousins were swept onto the crowded dance floor.

Indeed, Isabella thought, the mob before the doors was but a preamble to the one inside. Her partner was just as she had feared. Certainly he seemed all that was proper for one who was destined for a rural parsonage, and quite dull in the bargain, despite the mysterious quality that his black half-mask gave him.

His relative lack of conversation did give her some opportunity to look about apprehensively for the mysterious scion of the House of Sandleford. *My, perhaps it is like a novel.* The thought quirked her coral lips into a slight smile, which quite coincidentally arrived at the same moment as an attempted sally by her partner. Tremendously pleased and encouraged by the effect, he attempted several more until that smile became rather stiff.

Fortunately, the next dance was a waltz and her partner was compelled to deposit her at Mrs. de Clercy's side. Isabella secretly hoped that she might dance one later on the evening with another partner, but it would have been considered rather fast to dance one so early, even for a young lady in her second Season. Or so she told her forlorn partner, since he could not after all, hope to claim her hand for more than two dances without causing comment. Propriety was so useful at times, she reflected cheerfully as the future parson meandered disconsolately away.

As she sat conversing with Mrs. de Clercy, she felt that she exercised great restraint by not craning her neck in a vulgar manner to search the crowd. It had come to her that perhaps if Frederick Sandleford was here and was, in point of fact, Olivia's brother, then Olivia herself might be in Bath as well. That one thought quickly overcame all her embarrassment over her rude behavior earlier. She simply must be presented to the gentleman, somehow in this sea of masked dancers, and ask.

As her thoughts circled about this seemingly vain hope, she became so intent on trying to recognize him in the throng that the appearance of the gentleman at her very elbow came as something of a shock. She concealed her start with some difficulty. He was attired in the tightly cinched coat that was so fashionable among young men this Season, and a black silk half-mask like most of the other men present. In short, there was nothing to make her heart race as it did before Mrs. Grayson herself, the current queen of the Bath Ton, presented him as "Sir Frederick Sandleford."

This introduction alone told Isabella all that she needed to know regarding the mysterious gentleman's social connections, as did the murmur that danced through the surrounding mamas and others obliged by age or circumstances to sit out the dancing. Now their conversation would be remarked upon. *How provoking*, she thought as he led her to the floor.

The dark eyes twinkled merrily at her across the set while his mouth remained fixed in a supercilious expression. It brought her to mind of the highway robber, a thought which she attempted to thrust resolutely aside. "I am compelled to ask you, sir, if you have a sister named Olivia?" her voice trembled as she was turned gracefully and they ducked beneath the upstretched arms of the couple before them for the next figure of the dance.

"Indeed, I do," he responded with a slight bow, not meeting her eyes.

She nearly stumbled, green eyes so alive with joy that she forgot her fears for a moment. "Oh, pray, tell me, sir, is she well? Is she here in Bath? We were at school together. I long to see her more than anything else in the world!"

He bowed politely and favored her with a small smile as she was led away by the next figure. They were soon brought back together by the motion of the circle. "You shall, for I know that she is quite particular about wanting to see you as well." He looked up now, meeting her eyes with an unreadable expression that made her drop her gaze and look away. Oh, if only she had thought to bring a fan to hide her blushes!

"It must be very dull for you to be so far from London, particularly if you are compelled to chaperone your sister," she faltered through her attempted jest, forcing herself to look up and meet his eyes.

"I do find the charms of Bath quite make amends for the loss of the elegance of London." Here, he pressed her hand to his lips for just an instant too long. The intensity of the dark-eyed gaze under the long lashes left her no room for doubt as to his thoughts, and she hated herself for blushing. Indeed, he was so very like Olivia as to leave her with the most conflicted emotions, making her quite silent until the end of the dance.

"The room is over hot. May I, perhaps, escort the lady to the ices and have the honor of fetching her one?" he offered, his light tenor meant for her ears alone.

Those delicate shells turned an ever more dangerous shade of pink as Isabella nodded her acquiescence. He escorted her to an unoccupied chair near the window that was clearly in view of Mrs. de Clercy. Then he vanished into the throng around the ice table, managing to emerge unscathed at her side a mere instant before her previous partner could approach. An elegant, if stiff, bow soon discouraged the future parson who smothered his disappointment by going off to ask Emily to dance.

"Is your sister in Bath?" Isabella began with enthusiasm. "Oh, I simply must see her! I feared her perished," she paused a moment, silenced by the burning look in the dark eyes so near her own. Suddenly, they seemed very much those of the highwayman on the road, and not of the elegant young gentleman from the Pump Room at all. She shivered slightly under that masked gaze but was determined not to look away.

"I must tell you that she is well at present, but I fear greatly for her future. The fortunes of our family are not as they were." In response, Isabella arched one dark eyebrow above her mask, recalling his style of dress, which spoke of the services of an excellent tailor.

"I am not as I seem," he began again softly.

There was no further question in Isabella's mind. "I believe, sir, that we made your acquaintance on the road several days past," she spoke coldly.

"For the love you bore my sister, please let me explain!" This last comment caught the attention of those around them, and several ladies deep in conversation with each other suddenly had but little to say. Isabella met his eyes. A small drop hovered at the edge of one melting brown eye. How like his sister he was! Her common sense shrank from continuing while her heart urged her forward. They warred a moment. He caught her hand, occupied though it was by a spoon, and turned it to plant a warm kiss on the inside of her wrist.

This was no longer seemly and she drew herself up indignantly, even as her heart fluttered in guilty pleasure. "Please," he offered quietly, "let me walk with you on the Promenade tomorrow and I will tell you everything. There is something I must ask you after I have told you all."

She nodded cautiously, her embarrassment forgotten in curiosity and he escorted her back to Mrs. de Clercy. That good lady was more than happy to give her permission for him to call the next morning, and he vanished into the crowd with a graceful bow.

It may be conjectured as to the state of turmoil in which Isabella passed the rest of the evening. She remembered little of what passed, save the look of a certain pair of dark eyes and the brush of soft lips on her wrist. Her subsequent partners found her inattentive to their attempts at distraction and few sought more than one dance.

Mrs. de Clercy patted her hand with great meaning and Emily and Clara gave her encouraging and significant smiles as they swept by. Indeed, as they were quite the most popular young ladies in the Rooms that evening they were well content to congratulate their cousin on her more obvious conquest.

The sleepless night that she passed upon their return to Laura Place left Isabella with few of her natural defenses when Sir Frederick came to call the next morning. She blushed like a schoolgirl when her cousins teased her, much to their great amusement. Clara and Emily, serving as rather dubious chaperones, made sure to walk ahead of the two when the party ventured outside, sensing as they did that tender emotions might be the outcome of such a walk. He offered his arm and Isabella took it while avoiding meeting his eyes as she had since he arrived and they walked in silence for a brief time.

"I know you have recognized me as Olivia's brother," he began, "but there is more that you must know. Therefore, I must presume upon your friendship with my sister. Pray forgive my want of delicacy, I beg you. Our father perished in Brazil last year, and we were compelled to return to England. Our cousin took charge of my father's estate, and now allows my family only the meanest of livings. Until I marry, I have no legal right to our land or holdings. This is how you came to meet me on the road some days past. I have no trade, and my cousin will not buy an officer's commission for me. Even if that were possible," the last he muttered softly aside, causing Isabella's brows to quirk slightly and an unvoiced suspicion to fill her mind once more.

She looked at him sidelong, studying his face with its tan, slightly sunken cheeks covered by the long dark side whiskers. Her heart leapt a moment, then subsided. No, it was simply impossible, and she pushed her thought aside until he finished. "Without the gains that my activity brings to my family, they would be turned onto the highway, even from the shabby housing that we now share. So I am forced to lead a double life: gentleman of leisure who is above suspicion, and rogue who relieves gentlemen of their gold and ladies of their jewels."

Tears came to Isabella's eyes at the plight of her beloved Olivia's brother. With an effort she controlled her sympathies in favor of the common sense that she so valued. "Could you not marry without your cousin's permission, shocking though that would be?"

"Ah the lady that would agree to such a match would be a rarity indeed! To forego a wedding blessed by both our families for a flight to Gretna Green," he responded thoughtfully, "would be too much to ask of any gently bred lady of my acquaintance. No, I fear it cannot be." He stole a glance at his companion above his starched collar points.

Isabella pondered. He, seeing at once her level of distraction, chose to turn the conversation to Brazil, the state of the roads and other more suitable topics as they walked. One clear solution to the dilemma occurred to both but neither spoke of it, choosing to grant their distracted admiration to the glories of Bath instead. Clara and Emily dawdled ahead as much as they could decently do, but were soon compelled to join them by the crowds of the fashionable now filling the cobbled streets. All confidence at an end for the day, Isabella resigned herself to polite commonplace until they returned home.

The next morning, Sir Frederick appeared before the house in a handsome gig, hoping to gain the de Clercy's approval for a drive. Once given, though somewhat reluctantly, the sturdy bay horse soon had them on their way out to the edge of town. "My deeply held regret is that I cannot play the Nonesuch, hurrying you through town in style," he offered at her slightly startled look at his dignified pace. "I'm afraid my clothes show me more of a regular out-and-outer than my driving," he continued, steering the horse deftly around a tavern dray.

What an odd thing for a Pink of the Ton to admit, she thought, eyebrows quirking upward in a look which would have earned reproof from Mrs. de Clercy. There were so many things about him that reminded her of his sister. So very much, in fact, that it often seemed almost as though he actually *was* Olivia. She tried unsuccessfully to smother her impatience to travel swiftly to her long absent friend's side. The warmth that filled her at the thought of Olivia being so close vied with her frustration, driving her to the brink of impropriety by speaking the thought out loud.

She surveyed her companion as he wove through the farmers' carts at the edge of town, taking them out onto the curving road that wandered into the green fields outside Bath. Her mind was made up. Isabella became at that moment the daughter of her mother, a champion of a lady's right to be unconventional. With nary a further sensible thought about the consequences of her actions, she burst out, "Would you have my hand? I will do anything for Olivia! Anything to spare her from such a grim picture as you have painted!"

He stopped the horse, and gave her a startled glance as if to see if she spoke in jest. The reins dropped as his eyes lit up and he clasped her hands in his. "You are as brave as I remembered! I mean as Olivia has always said you were," he continued in a rush. "I would be honored to have your hand in marriage. But we must do it in secret, else my cousin will intervene to stop us."

He had more to say, and before Isabella quite knew what had happened, she had agreed to a tryst in the garden to be followed by a late night flight to Gretna, where they could be married without a license.

Emily and Clara met them upon their return and noted their cousin's high color with favor. Indeed her very eyes danced with excitement. To be a sister to Olivia and to see her each day! The joy of the thought quite overcame any hesitation she felt at the suddenness of this turn of events.

The Misses turned discreetly away for a moment, giving Sir Frederick the opportunity to press her hand to his lips once more. Isabella dreamily met his eyes and found that she longed to meet his lips as she had once met Olivia's. They were so very alike, she thought as he ardently kissed the palm of one dainty hand and closed the fingers against the spot as though to hold the kiss in her hand.

She dwelt on that thought as she prepared a farewell note to the de Clercys. Much as she wished to entrust them with this secret, she could not suppress a concern that they would attempt to stop her. While she had no wish to insult their concern for her well being, she could not bear the thought of Olivia, her lovely face aged and broken, turned from her home and begging by the wayside.

In truth, she found that her good sense had been quite undermined by the look in a certain pair of brown eyes and the gentle touch of warm lips. She was quite unable to truly consider other options than the one they had decided upon. Time enough to patch the vase once it was broken, her mother used to say, and so she would, determined to call on her cousins after their return from Scotland and beg their forgiveness.

Nearly oblivious to those around her, she claimed to have the headache and retired early to her room that evening. Her young cousins exchanged glances of great significance but said little as she went slowly up the stairs. She ate her supper in her room rather than face her relatives in her current state of mind.

Cool, practical Isabella! She mocked herself as she packed two small bandboxes with essential items. Then, she sat down by the window to wait, only getting up to pace as little as every few minutes or so.

When the midnight hour struck and all was still, she ventured into the passage and slipped as silently as possible down the servants' stairs. At the garden gate, she paused a moment. "Here now, miss," Sophie appeared behind her as she stifled a scream. "Let me carry those for you."

Isabella angrily whispered, "What are you doing here?"

"Miss Clara seemed to think you were up to something and tipped me a guinea to keep a weather eye out for you, and sure enough, here you are, just as she said. She was concerned about your reputation, as I don't mind saying so, you should be as well. He is a-going to marry you, is he not, miss?" The maid fixed Isabella with a stern eye.

Isabella nodded mutely, horrified at having given herself away. "Very well, then, I don't see as how I can stop you, and no doubt you've got your reasons, so let's be off. I can see the carriage in the lane," said Sophie in resigned tones. "And no point in giving me the slip, either, Miss. There's another guinea in it for me if I bring you back with your new husband for a wedding dinner. I just hope you know what you're doing," she added dryly. Isabella couldn't prevent a rueful smile from curling her lips. There was nothing for it but to go.

Frederick waited to hand her up into the chaise and four that waited at the end of the garden. He raised an eyebrow at the sight of Sophie, but accepted Isabella's whispered explanation. Once inside, they were off to Scotland with a clatter.

Isabella sat across from him and studied his face, seemingly so dear and so familiar in the moonlight. In truth, his resemblance to his sister was even more uncanny when he no longer played the dandy. But what did she truly know of him? What would it be like to be married to such a man? she wondered drowsily. Sophie began to snore gently beside her as he glanced away from the window and smiled at her.

"Belle, if I may call you so? There is something that I must say before we are too far from Bath. I meant to tell you yesterday, but found that cowardice held my tongue." He drew a deep breath, closing his eyes for a moment. Isabella felt her heart give way. "I'm not Frederick Sandleford." Isabella's hands tightened on her reticule in a rush of warm feeling, somewhat akin to relief. Then he had to be… "Frederick died in the same accident that killed our father. I am…"

"Olivia!" Isabella finished with a rush. She found that it was not the surprise that it might have been. However, a certain obstacle heretofore unconsidered presented itself. "But how then can we be married?" She paused in thought, "Am I the only one in your confidence?"

"Only you and my dear mama. No one has guessed my secret, fortunately not even our cousin." Olivia looked into Isabella's lovely green eyes. Isabella drew forward, almost without knowing what she did. A lurch of the coach threw her into Olivia's arms. They embraced and kissed ardently.

"Here now, time enough for all that after you're wed," Sophie grumbled sleepily from her corner.

"Will you still have me, dearest?" Olivia gazed into Isabella's eyes and found her answer there. Isabella thought, as her lips pressed Olivia's once more, how glad she was that Miss Havershere had been right all along.

Vadija

I have heard it said that even Vadija the Merry could not lift the sorrows from Laith. In all the tales the sadness swam sluggishly through the streets of the city like the giant carp in the slow moving River Omphere or the mist clouds from the Kaleva Mountains. Each inhabitant carried the city's misery balanced precariously on their packs or on their bare shoulders as they walked the gray avenues, one foot dragging up to collapse down in front of the other.

So it was said. Said with a kind of pride, at that. But I didn't believe it. I had heard that the city wasn't a happy place, mind you. But I knew that Vadija had a merry and glorious laugh, a laugh that changed things. They said it was like a clarion call to arms, if you were a soldier, and liked being one. Or the wind whipping through the Forest of Anma Bekash, if you were a hunter. Once Puar the money-lender even said to me "Ah, Sira, her laugh is like a rain of gold coins poured down a chimney and ringing on the stones below." From her, this was the highest of praise.

I thought I heard Vadija laugh once myself before I heard her name. The sound rode down on the wind and sang around the chimney of my farm, making the little bells on the door ring and the dogs howl with the shock of it. Swirling and roaring, it swept around me until I came near to howling myself. I didn't know what it was then, but I left that day. There was nothing to hold me once I heard it. Her laugh is like that.

But even she couldn't change Laith of the Sorrows, or so they told me as I followed the news of her laughter from my distant valley and days of unending work. Always she went a little before me and I had to make my own way. But I kept walking for I had no laugh of my own in those days. I thought she might tell me how she found hers.

In the beginning, I washed and cleaned at the inns and little farms to keep bread in my pack and a roof over my head. I told tales to the children back then, for they were the only ones who heard them. When I could, I sat and listened to the rare talespinner who would venture so far from the cities of the coast, letting the words wash over me and wondering always where they had found such things.

It was then I first heard Vadija's name and learned that it was her laughter that drew me from my home. But though I listened until I could repeat the tales, I had no thought to become a talespinner myself, not at first. Certainly I knew I could not be one because everyone said that I was not the way a talespinner should be. After all, talespinners are long and lean where I am soft and round, dark where I am golden, mysterious where I am open and speak what I mean. So it was said. But sometimes when I thought those things, I remembered Vadija's laugh. Then all things seemed possible.

As I traveled, I began to see words growing in the hedges and drifting on the breeze. It terrified me at first, for I knew no one else who could see them. I tried to ignore them, turning away from the small whispers of sound and the touch of dreams.

But soon I could see them even while I slept. They led me through the dreamlands and my waking days until I could stand it no more and I reached out to one, touching it. Then another. I called them to me and they came. I was no longer afraid.

With the words I began to weave the webs that drew in those who listened. One night, a circle at the fire followed me up the Princess of Velena's rainbow stairs. I made the steps glisten with color and shine with the firelight's glow in the eyes of those who heard until I could see them myself. The next night, another circle swam behind me with Gregoth of the Sea, gasping at the vengeance that he wrecked on those who slew his people, and at the sudden tang of salt in the air.

After that, I began to tell stories at the inns and wayside traveler's rests. These were tales about strange lands and mighty warriors, like those I told my little ones before the wasting fever carried them off. Lord Death took them, just as he had taken their father before them, and I could do nothing but watch. Until I heard Vadija, I wished that he had taken me, too.

I found my tales hard to tell at first, but the words kept flowing around me and I went with them until I could no more stop telling stories than I could stop following Vadija. After a while, I even made up new tales. Kingdoms fell, lovers were reunited, evil was conquered: such was the stuff of the stories that I told. I began to feel joy in the telling of what could be and what should not, and soon I had a small laugh of my own.

But my tales about Vadija were best of all, at least to me, and they came to me often when I walked or when I washed and tended. I told them to the women and children and those who were worn from their day's work. In those stories, she laughed and armies crumbled. Tyrants flew away on the wind. Always her laugh changed things for the best. So I said and so I believed though I had done nothing but follow her trail, never once laying eyes on her.

Still, I talked to many on the road who had heard her laugh. Some of them even claimed to have seen her. She was young or old, lean or fat, beautiful beyond a winter's frost on lacy tree branches, or ugly and grim like the burning lava in the mountains on the southern edge of the world, depending on who told me the story.

I had my own idea, held close within me with the tales that I told no one else. I knew that she must be a big, queenly woman with strong arms and a great soft belly, bigger even than my own. For how else could she have the power to laugh such a laugh that changed those who heard it? But I didn't know so I looked for her to see for myself. Before I heard her, I never could have wanted such a thing

After a time, people began to know my name and my tales kept my belly round though I walked leagues each day, following the trail she left behind her. Finally, her path turned toward Laith of the Sorrows, a city out of legend, and there I went also.

It was midday when I arrived and stood before the walls. I paused and trembled outside the gates long before I was willing to follow her inside.

There were many tales of how Laith gained its sorrows. In some, they sacrificed their children to one of the Old Gods to save themselves from siege. In others, they betrayed their king and brought his curse down upon them. At the end of each story, they were left gray and solemn, bereft of joy and music for season turn to season turn from my grandmere's time onward. I remembered each story as I paused between the cold metal gates before stepping forward. They closed with a bang to swallow me as I set foot on the flagstones of Laith.

Once inside, I could see no more of the lands outside for Laith's sorrows are sealed in by the high walls. There were no inns and no other places where people could gather to hear my tales so instead I walked through the city looking for Vadija.

As I searched, the gray walls to each side and the gray paving stones beneath my feet sent icy fingers through me and I shivered, warm though my cloak was. The sun's dim light barely lit my way as those who lived in this place shouldered past me, unseeing, and my heart grew colder and colder.

When I had wandered some time down the long avenues where not a single flower bloomed, I could feel the wings of the city's sorrows settling around my shoulders. "Why, why did she come here?" I wailed in a whisper, fearing to speak aloud and draw the misery closer. I could see no one who could be her in the dismal faces that passed me but I knew she must be here somewhere. There was nowhere else for her to go unless she flew over the mountains that circled the city on three sides. Besides, a voice whispered inside me, how could she deny such pain? Or such a challenge? How I longed then to have her power!

I tried to ignore my thoughts and listened hard for her laugh, but there was nothing. No chime of bells or dogs barking or normal city sounds. I could hear only the creak of passing wagons the color of twilight and the soft, whispered exchanges between the few merchants and those who bought from them. The words were so soft that none fell to the cold hard ground, so light that no tales could grow from them.

The weight of despair settled heavier and heavier upon my shoulders until I had to sit or fall to my knees. I sank onto a cold step, cursing Vadija for coming here and myself for following her. My tales began to fade when I did this, gliding away like water with no basin left to hold it. How long I sat this way I do not know, for the hours pass strangely in Laith of the Sorrows. Soon there was no joy left in me and I began to forget Vadija's laugh and the world beyond the city walls.

Still I sat and drifted until I gazed at nothing but the gray stones beneath my feet. After a great while, I knew that someone stood before me, but by then I had not even the strength to look up. "Outlander, you must leave this place," the voice whispered down at me like a breeze. I knew that what it said was right but I could not lift my head to go. A gnarled hand clasped my shoulder hard but it was nothing compared to the despair that held me and I scarcely felt it.

The hand reached down for my own and tugged upward until I was dragged unwillingly to my feet. The bony fingers reached under my chin and forced my eyes up to meet those of an old, old woman, her face gray and drained like the others I had seen. But her eyes were different. In their black depths, I could see a tale growing, a story of gray and cold, but a story nonetheless.

"Tell me what you seek, Outlander," her voice licked at my hearing like a small wind, like a sigh.

I tried to remember and all that came to me was my dream of Vadija, and I saw her as I imagined that she must be. She did not laugh, not here in this twilight place, and she shrank in size with the loss. I shrank with her, folding in around the vision, bright garments dimming. She was little more than I had been before I left the farm, and the sight pained me. "I was looking for Vadija," I whispered back to the woman, tears rolling down my cheeks.

"I thought you might be," the dark eyes twinkled slightly and I found that I could lift my head on my own, without the support of her hand. I still had no words, no tales to tell until she spoke again, "Tell me about her, talespinner."

I wondered how she could see the words to know me for what I was until I looked and saw those that had fallen to the gray stones around me. Many were fading away, but a small few still glowed brightly against the dim light and the cold. "Vadija…" I stumbled over her name but I whispered on, coaxing the few remaining words back to me, remembering a tale that I had told no one else. "Vadija came once to a valley far from here. There, I heard I her laugh for the first and only time." The woman's sparkling eyes were closed for a moment.

"What did the valley look like, talespinner?"

I told her what I could still remember of my home and my family. Sometimes the words came to me and sometimes I made new ones as I told her the tale of how I had come to seek Vadija. With each turning of the tale's web, I could feel the city's sorrow loosen its grip upon us both. She wore the ghost of a smile and I stood on my own, my voice more than a whisper, growing in strength. There was a wind now that night had fallen, and though it was a cold one, I welcomed it and the words that it brought.

She asked me many questions as we stood shivering in that wind and twice the merchant on whose steps we sat came forth to drive us away, but was terrified by the strangeness of that which she did not know and retreated inside.

With each answer and each word, I grew warmer until I slipped my cloak from my shoulders. It was then that I saw the little blossom growing in a crack between the gray stones, drawing itself up from where my tears had fallen. It was but one against all that gray expanse, but it was enough.

I pointed to it and laughed. It was just a little laugh but I saw the woman's eyes grow wide at hearing it and she smiled a little. I laughed again for the small joys of seeing her smile and the tiny flower struggling against the sad city. The wind caught the sound this time and sent it upward to dash against the gray stone walls and the closed windows of Laith. The stone sent my laugh back, flinging it between the wind and the stone until I saw the chink of windows and doors opening as those who lived in the city looked out to see what was wrong.

The bits and pieces of my laugh danced around them on the wind and they drew back, many of them, retreating into the gray insides of their chilled homes. Only one, a young man with dead eyes, came out to stand beside the woman. His glance fell upon the flower and upon the words that lay on the stone and he blinked slowly, carefully, as though trying to understand what they meant. I wondered that one with eyes so dead could see the words, but perhaps he did not.

He reached out to the flower at my feet and pulled it up. Its delicate beauty vanished in a moment and he held a gray blossom in his palm. His face opened somewhat in astonishment, then closed as he laid the flower back at my feet. Without a word, he turned and walked back into his house, and his door and all the others that remained open shut against the small remains of my laugh and the tiny petals of the gray flower.

I met the eyes of the old woman, and found their gentle spark fading. "He does not need your gift yet," she whispered softly, but I did not understand. I tried to force a laugh, but it would not come. The cold crept up my limbs, tendrils reaching once again from the stones beneath my feet to root me to the spot. My spirit cried out for Vadija, but still I heard nothing until at last, I grew angry with cold and loss.

I threw my head back and I howled her name out upon the wind that carried no more words. Once more, it dashed my voice upon the walls and flung it at the city gates at the far end of the street. Wearily, they swung open, but I could see no one standing outside, waiting to be swallowed by the city.

Quickly, I grabbed the old woman's hands and marched down the street pulling her unresisting behind me. If Vadija would not come to me, then I would wait for her at the city gates until she emerged. So said the voice of my anger as it buzzed and crackled around my ears. How dared she do this to me, dragging me from hearth and home to this place? The despair that I had left with the telling of my tale began to return, but I fought it until we reached the gates.

Here, the woman stopped and would go no further. "I can't leave."

The whisper made me pause in my headlong rush to leave the city behind me. "Why not?" I demanded as I bathed my eyes in view of the lands beyond the city gate.

"Because I built this place, I and all the others. It is part of us and we of it. I must stay and help those who want to leave weave tales of their own. There is nothing for me there," she gestured at the lands outside. In my anger and my astonishment, I threw back my head and I laughed, a harsh noise in that quiet place.

She flinched away from the brittle hardness of the sound which dashed like ice on the wind, tinkling against the stone walls and shattering. For a moment, I was tall and lean and mysterious, as it was said a talespinner should be. My laugh rose until bitter tears flowed down my cheeks and I sought outside for the words that would break the stone wall, for I wanted to succeed in my anger where Vadija had not in her merriment.

"Please don't." I barely heard her speak, but it was enough. I stopped laughing and looked at her. Then I was short and round, though not as merry and frank as I had been since I began to follow Vadija. The old woman stood before me, thin shoulders bowed with the weight of the city's grief, but still with a little light in her eyes for those who could see it. Now I began to understand. I knew where Vadija came from. With a small shove, the woman pushed me outside the city gates and backed away from them as they began to close once more, sealing her in.

The lands beyond called me, their words caressing my face and pulling me back to them, but I stood instead for a time looking upon the walls of Laith of the Sorrows. As I stood my laugh grew strong within me, filling me with tales, and I could feel myself grow with them until I was rounder and taller than I had been before I came to here.

I thought about my children and my husband and the man with the dead eyes and I wept then, the tears pouring down my cheeks in a steady stream until a small creek flowed away from my feet. Tiny flowers sprang up against the walls of the city and I laughed once more, even in my sorrow, and I grew no smaller.

Long I sat and thought about what had been and what could be until I looked to the lands beyond the city. I thought of a funny story that Puar the moneylender had told me, a simple tale unworthy of a talespinner, but with a light of its own. I thought too of the old woman with her listening eyes and of what she had asked. After a while, I knew that I didn't need to see Vadija anymore. I went away then without loosening my merriment against the grim walls.

My laugh went on before me on the wind, whipping away to ring around the chimneys of small farms and knocking on the doors of tyrants. But always it went ahead, never behind to the city that I left. For it was said that even Vadija the Merry could not lift the sorrows from Laith. So it was said and so it would be.

A Scent of Roses

The night it is gude Halloween,
The faery folk do ride,
And they that wad their true-love win,
At Miles Cross they maun bide.
—*Tam Lin*, traditional ballad

Janet straightened her back against the persistent ache that filled her and wiped the sweat from her brow with a grimy hand. The sun was setting slowly, blinding her until she looked away. Time to leave the field and go back to the cottage. She grimaced at the thought. Tam would no doubt have been at the ale. He'd sit by the fire again tonight, singing that witch's tongue the Good Folk spoke and telling her tales about their country as if she cared to know.

With a groan, she picked up her hoe and her bag and began the weary walk home. Almost she wished that she'd not lain with him in the rose garden of her father's house at Carterhaugh. Almost she wished that her courage had failed at the crossroads marked by Miles Cross and that she had not saved him from the Fair Folk. But wishing would not take her back in time, nor restore their babe, sickened and dead in his cradle a year past. If he had lived, her father might have accepted Tam as his heir. Instead, he exiled her and her faery knight to a distant holding, little more than a cottage and a few rocky fields. She kicked at a rock in her path, wincing when it hurt her toes through her thin shoes.

"No longer so proud as you once were, I see."

The voice was cool and sardonic but it fell on Janet's ears like a burning brand. She spun around to face her tormentor but the words caught in her throat. A lady sat on a great stone by the side of the path and her face Janet could never forget. "You!" She spat. "Have you not had revenge enough but must needs come back to mock me in my fall?"

The other woman tilted her head sideways like a bird, but no bird had eyes so fearsome and strange. Janet could not hold back a shiver and the Queen of the Fair Folk smiled to see it. "You fear me now, mortal? I was not so fearsome when you stole my knight away."

"Would your Majesty care to try and take him back?" Janet's fists clenched and her cheeks flushed red. She dropped her tools at her feet, bracing herself as if to box.

The Queen threw back her head with a merry tinkling laugh. "If I did not kill you then, why would I brawl with you like one of your fishwives now? You won him fair, Janet, and he is yours to mind and tend."

"Then why are you here?" Janet asked, her voice uncertain. "I've kine to tend and bairns and Tam to feed. You've naught to do with me."

"Do I not?" The Queen stood, her gown of green falling to her feet like a river of grass. She seemed taller than Janet remembered and she flinched away, as afraid now as she had been two years before. "There are no bairns, as you know well. Naught but my former knight waits for you and he sleeps before the fire, an empty cup by his chair."

Janet's blood ran hot again. "Tis your fault! If you had not taken him, he would be an honored knight at the King's court! We should have had bairns aplenty and lands and…" Here her voice broke and she wiped savagely at her eyes.

The Queen reached out her hand, her skin glowing a pale green in the dim light. With one feather light touch, she captured one of Janet's tears and brought it to her lips. She gave Janet a hard stare for a breath or two. Then her face softened in an odd smile, one that made her look a bit like any village girl watching her swain.

In a trice, she was gone, vanished like a dream. Janet stared at the spot where she had stood, one hand clasping the cheek those faery fingers had touched. Her skin burned pleasantly, sending a heat through her that she'd not felt in far too long. She took a deep breath and realized that the air around her was full of the scent of the roses of Carterhaugh.

Torn between anger and something she dared not examine too closely, she picked up her hoe and bag and resumed her walk home. Now it was growing dark and the trees' branches twined an arch across the path above her head. All around her the evening was filled with small sounds: the cry of the hunting owl, the soft crackle of a deer's hooves on fallen leaves, and above it all, the distant silver tinkle of bells like those on a bridle. Would the Queen return for her? The thought made her flee for the safety of the cottage, shivering.

She slammed the door behind her and dropped the bolt in place before she turned to look around her, heart racing. Tam sat just as she knew he would: handsome sleeping face lit by the dying flames and an empty jug beside him. As she watched, he blinked and sat up, blue eyes puzzled as if he had dreamt of other times and places. Perhaps his dreams were full of eyes that had no color Janet could name.

Anger filled her with the thought, driving out the fear that held her silent in the doorway. “You drunken sot! Have you done nothing but lay here all day? Did you even go to the castle to see if Lord Edmond would have you as a guard?” She stalked toward the fire without waiting for an answer, for she knew there would be none that would please her.

“Ah Janet, lass, you know they’ll have none of me up at the castle. Better I should come to the fields with you and work the soil at your side.” He ran trembling fingers through his brown curls, leaning forward so his elbows rested on his knees.

“You cannot till the soil, and the cattle tremble when they see you. You are good for nothing but the sword and the lute and pleasing the Fair Folk’s Queen until she saw fit to tithe you to Hell!” As soon as the words were spoken, Janet wished she could call them back.

Tam Lin gave her a look of pure agony, all cloudiness gone from the blue glory of his eyes for a moment. She felt his pain as if it was her own and she dropped a gentle hand to his shoulder as she went to stoke the fire. It was not all his fault that he was not raised to the farm and that the castle would not have him. Yet if he would try harder and drink less, they might yet make their living from this farm and the herd her father gave them as a parting gift. She sighed, wondering if she must fight the battle anew tonight.

Instead, he stood unsteadily. “I’ll fetch the kine.”

“No, Tam, they fear you. I’ll do it.” She turned toward the door, remembering her earlier terror with a start.

He was there before her, wordlessly unbarring the door and vanishing into the darkness beyond. She started to follow him, then changed her mind and went to put on the remains of the morning’s porridge for their dinner. Perhaps the beasts would grow accustomed to him with time. Unthinking, her hand caressed her cheek as if the Queen's fingertips were still there. She watched the fire for a span of breaths, seeing a beautiful face out of dream instead of her humble cauldron.

She was still standing there when Tam came back from stabling the cattle. He barred the door quietly and came up behind her to wrap his arms tight around her waist. She could feel his lips in her hair as he held her, desire stirring sluggishly inside her as if waking from a long sleep. She smiled at him over one shoulder, then swung the pot of porridge away from the fire before turning to kiss him. When they paused for breath, some impulse made her whisper, "Do you still dream about her?"

Tam pulled away from her as if stung. "Why must you ask these questions? You won me, heart and soul. Must you have all my thoughts as well?"

Janet gaped at him and stammered, "I only…" She stopped at his upraised palm and the shake of his head. Perhaps there had been too many words already tonight. Silently, she ladled the porridge into the wooden bowls and equally silently, they ate. Little more passed between them until Janet, weary of the silence heavy with unspoken thoughts, went to their bed alone leaving Tam to brood before the dying fire.

The dreams that came to her that night would have seen her barred from their humble church. The Queen rode through each of them, the bells jingling at her horse's bridle to signal her coming. Each dream began with her touch, sometimes her fingers on Janet's cheek, sometimes her lips. As the night wore on, her fingers and lips tasted Janet's breast and her tongue traced the outline of her belly. Then the curved roundness of her thighs. Janet started awake before that tongue could go elsewhere, sitting up to gasp for air and shudder at the burning in her loins.

Beside her, Tam slept like the dead, hearing and feeling nothing of her distress. She put out a tentative hand and rested it on his bare shoulder, then lay down at his side, pressing close against him. How could she want such things? Surely, this was the Devil's work and she was under a glamour. The Queen had tasted her tears. That must be how she did it. Tomorrow, she must go to the kirk and beg for shriving. Only that could save her soul. She lay awake, listening to Tam's heavy breathing and shivering under the burden of her thoughts until dawn.

"I must go to the priest," she told Tam when the cows were fed and they had eaten their meal. "Will you come with me?"

He shook his head but did not meet her eyes. "The damned fool will scrub all with holy water if he sees me. I cannot bear the stench of fear and hatred that hangs about the old man. Today I will feed the cattle and go to the field." His jaw was set and his face was grim when he described these simple tasks and Janet could not help letting a small sigh escape her lips. A quick and furious glare came hard on its heels to meet her eyes, then Tam caught up the tools and was gone.

She bit back the impulse to tell him not to lose the cows or burn down the cottage. It would do no good and was best left unsaid. At least it was better than that he should spend the day awash in ale. She was off to the kirk then. Still she found that her feet moved but slowly down the path despite her resolution. The old priest was foolish, just as Tam said. Perhaps he did not have the power to stand against a glamour like this. "Do you want him to?" The unspoken question whispered against her ear like a soft breeze carrying the breath of a lover.

Janet trembled against the words, the heat of strange longing filling her until she was near to feeling the Queen's lips against her own. She fought it with a howl more like an animal's than her own voice. "Yes!" When the word passed her lips, she dropped to her knees in the grass and prayed as she had never done before. Desperation lent her thoughts an earnest fervor that cooled her heated limbs and drove all dreams from her until she could stand and resume her walk. It would be enough. The priest would shrive her and there would be no more dreams, no phantom touches to give her unclean thoughts.

But the old priest was nowhere to be found when she reached the church. When she asked in the village, one had him at a deathbed in the Highlands, another at a baptism in a village some hours walk away. Discouraged, she went into the tiny church and knelt in prayer for a time. She could not say how long her head was bowed, how hard it was to send her thoughts toward heaven but when she stood at last, she swayed with hunger and the priest had still not returned.

She made her way out and followed the stream that ran through the churchyard away from the village. She walked until she reached a clearing ringed with berry bushes nearly past their full ripeness. These she added to the hard bread she had brought in her pocket and the water from the stream. Then she sat a time, watching the water flow past.

Her thoughts unbidden turned to Tam's tales of the Faery lands. Wild tales they were, full of a land in eternal spring, ever blooming and flourishing. There were green forests to ride through and clear streams to drink from and marvels to see with each passing day. The Queen's palace was made of silver and gems, flashing in the pale sunlight and all her folk were beautiful to hearts-breaking.

In all, he made it seem a paradise that she had kidnapped him from. Her jaw tightened with the thought. Once and once alone, he spoke of the other things he had seen there: the redcaps, the Jack-in-Irons with his clanking chains and the other nightmare creatures of fang and claw. They, too, dwelt in that fair land and haunted its corners and dark hollows, lying in wait for the unwary.

He spoke then too of the day he heard that the Court paid a tithe to Hell every seven years to keep them safe from the flames of God's wrath. The Fair Folk whispered that it must be he who went in place of them, for he had a soul and they had none. How he shuddered when he spoke of it! Janet herself shivered to remember it now, even in the warmth of the summer sun.

To drive the thought from her mind, she rose and went to the berry bushes. In the thicket was the biggest, juiciest berry she had ever seen and she reached for it, straining until her fingers clasped it. A thorn caught her then and she pulled her hand quickly from the bush as a bright red drop of blood spilled over her skin. She raised it to her lips only to feel the weight of another's gaze hard upon her. Janet whirled, heart racing, to find the Queen watching her from under a great oak tree a few paces away, a white horse at her side.

"Have you no servants, Madam, who can be trusted to spy on me but that you must do it yourself?" Janet asked when she caught her breath.

"Ah, but it pleases me to watch you. I stole Tam because he was brave and beautiful and bright with mortal promise, but you, you are something more." The Queen tilted her head as if considering what that might be.

Janet crossed herself frantically. If only the priest had been there to shrive her! She could not fail to notice that the gesture made the Queen smile and she shuddered, closing her eyes against desire and fear. Something caught her hand and she felt lips as tender as the dawn capture the blood welling from the scratch the thorns had left. All strength left her and she fell to her knees, heart pounding and flesh burning until her hand was released.

Then she forced herself to her feet and dragged her eyelids open. The Queen was far too close and Janet staggered back away from her, welcoming the bracing trunk of a giant oak at her back. The other's face had a glimmer of wonder in it. "You still resist me. Tam was mine for a fall from his horse into a mushroom ring, yet you can stand apart from me, despite what I have taken from you. I have never seen your like before, Janet. Can you still wonder that I come to try you myself instead of sending others?"

Janet shivered against the tree. "What glamour have you thrown on me, fiend?"

"I cast no spell. Come to me of your own free will, Janet, and I will show you all the wonders of Faery. Only come to Miles Cross to ride at my side on Hallows Eve." With one last near wistful smile, the Queen of the Fey vanished into the woods with only the faint jingle of bells and the frantic racing of Janet's heart left to mark her passage.

Janet seized her bag and took to her heels, running toward the village as fast as she could, her long skirt tangling in her legs. Only when she staggered into the churchyard could she bring herself to look at the scratch on her hand. The flesh had begun to heal itself under a gossamer web like a spider's. Staring at it in horror, she fled into the church, the priest's name on her lips. Her words echoed into emptiness and she fell sobbing on her knees before the altar.

It was anger, finally, that drove her to her feet and onto the path that led back to their cottage. It seemed God's reward for saving Tam's soul was to put her own in danger. Bitterly, she cursed the impulse that had led her to Miles Cross and the night that she first spied the Queen of the Fairies in her bold, bright fury. Would that she had left Tam to his fate and born his bastard in the comforting concealment of her father's castle. He would have married her off to one of his knights and she could have continued a life free from want and desire alike.

Frowning, she imagined a life without Tam or the Queen. The thoughts sat heavy on her shoulders until the cottage came into view and she quickened her pace to reach it. Enough of might-have-beens. She made her choices at Miles Cross and Carterhaugh and there was no more to it than that. Now she had the kine to tend and the porridge to make. Her cousin had even promised her a chicken and a rooster before winter came. They would make their own ease and if she loved Tam a little less for the life they now led, it was not so different from other married folk.

Her back was straight and firm and her jaw set in resolve when she entered the cottage. The fire was cold in the hearth, but at least there was no silent figure in the chair, no empty jug on the floor. Tam must still be abroad in the field. Well and good, she must be about her own chores then. With a will, she set to setting the cottage to rights, starting the fire anew and placing the pot on the flames to boil. The floor was swept and the cobwebs in the corners cleaned away with scarce a shudder when Tam returned from the field.

He looked weary and red with the sun but she could hear the cattle outside. All was well and her lips curved into a welcoming smile as she kissed his cheek. He gave her a startled look and a shy smile in return and so they sat down to their stew at the table. "Did the priest shrive you then?" He asked after a few moments' talk.

Janet jumped in her chair, her hand going to her cheek as if the Queen's fingers still lay there. She made herself shrug as if it was no great thing, as if her fears and wants were like the washing and the mending. "No. He was away in the Highlands. I will go back another day for shriving." Tam nodded and returned to his stew, leaving her lost in her thoughts.

That night, they tried to recover some of what they had lost in the warmth of kisses and hot skin against skin until they fell asleep wrapped in each other's arms. No dreams about the Queen came to trouble Janet that night or the next or the ones that followed.

Instead, she began to see herself as she would be ten, twenty years hence when hard work on the farm had taken its toll. By then, she feared that she and Tam would have no more love for each other but would remain together from long habit and fondness. A great emptiness filled Janet when she woke from these dreams and more and more her fingers stole to her cheek or to her hand. She remembered the wild elation of Miles Cross, the knowledge that she alone had succeeded in defying the Queen of the Faeries. She remembered feeling alive and the dreams that she had now were repugnant to her.

More than once, she tried to speak to Tam of it but the harder he worked in the fields, the more silent he became. Sometimes she found him polishing his old sword and once she saw him fight an opponent that none could see but him. His dreams at night seemed as troubled as her own but she found no words to ask him what he feared. Nor did she tell him anything of the Queen, though once she tried to get him to tell her about his time at her Court. He gave her a sharp look and asked. "What have you to do with mushroom rings and those that dance within them?"

"Nothing. I but remember the tales you told me before." She stumbled over the lie and she could see that he knew it for what it was. He said nothing more, only reaching over to press her hand, a look of pity in his eyes.

It was two mornings later that a well-dressed man rode up to their gate on a fine horse and spoke long with Tam. She heard none of their words and cared little more, thinking the stranger only a lost traveler. It was only when she came into the barn later to find Tam with his sword in his hands, his feet treading a measure with an imaginary opponent that she thought to ask, "Who was he? What did he say to you?" She sat on a pile of hay, admiring despite herself the sweep of the blade and the rusty grace with which he held it.

He spun, beheading a shadow before he rested the point of the blade on the dirt in front of him. "He came to speak to me of a fool's errand beyond the sea, of fighting and glory and all else that a farmer's life does not offer. He spoke of gold to be won, Janet, and a name to be regained." Tam did not meet her eyes, looking only at the sword in his hands. Even so, she could see that his eyes held a fire to them that she had not seen since Carterhaugh.

He put up the sword then, sliding it into its scabbard with an ease that his hands knew well. But she saw how his hand lingered on the hilt and she knew what his answer must be. She said nothing more, remembering with a start that tonight was Hallows Eve and Miles Cross was not so long a ride from the cottage. Her heart beat madly then for all she went about her work as though it was a day like any other. Tam, too, seemed lighter of heart but still they did not speak of their thoughts to each other.

And such thoughts they were! She shuddered at the tithe, bit back a wail at the thought of the monsters of Faery, of what she would leave behind. Still and all, what would she do with Tam gone, even if he sent back whatever gold he won? There was nothing for her here but to grow old and lonely and bitter until even the Queen of Faeries would have no use for her. But to live at the Queen's side, that would be worth the risks surely. Her thoughts ran round and round until dusk.

Her choice when it came found her running to the stable. She led their old plow horse out of the barn as quietly as she could. She had only just saddled the beast when there came Tam with his kit over one shoulder and his sword buckled at his side. They looked at each other for a long moment in the fading light until he spoke at last. "You go to her at Miles Cross, then?" He frowned, his hand reaching up to caress her cheek.

She held his hand there and kissed his palm. "And you away beyond the sea to fight?" He nodded and she smiled at him in understanding. Together, they released the cattle from the makeshift barn and doused the fire in the hearth. Together, they stood side by side looking at the cottage and the rocky fields around it.

Tam spoke first. "I loved you true, Janet, with no glamour to compel it. I will miss you." He pulled her close and held her tight. "Beware the tithe, love. If I may, I will come to Carterhaugh a year hence. If you need me, leave word for me there."

Janet wiped away a tear and smiled up at him. "Go well, love. May you be safe from all harm and find what you seek." Their lips met briefly in a final kiss. Then she mounted the old horse, glancing back to wave him on his way as they parted. Her heart almost failed her then and the night seemed full of secret sounds and whispers. Her hands trembled on the reins and she watched the shadows on either side. From far away, she heard music and laughter but she forced herself to stay on the path and closed her eyes so that she would not see whoever made the sounds. Still she rode on, turning neither to left nor right until the moon rose and the great stone cross appeared before her.

Then she had naught to do but wait for what seemed an eternity. When she had come to rescue Tam, she had hidden in the bushes, catching the Queen all unawares, but tonight she sat in full moonlight at the crossroads like a knight from a tale.

Before she had her love for Tam and their babe inside her to buoy her courage, but tonight she had nothing but her dreams and the very longings that she feared. Almost she turned her horse back, almost she rode for her father's court to ask his forgiveness. Always something held her there, waiting.

It was nearly midnight when she heard the jingle of bells on bridles and saw the glow of riders through the trees. Her heart beat so fast she thought it would jump out of her mouth and the old horse fidgeted beneath her as he caught her mood. The faery knights came closer, the ladies of the Seelie Court on their heels and she could see that their eyes shone with colors that she could not name and that they were beautiful to hearts-breaking. All fell silent to see her there and the faery riders came to a halt at the edge of the clearing. She stared back at them, a wild excitement rising in her.

The Queen came riding through her courtiers and smiled to see her waiting there. Something broke inside Janet, like a river when the thaw comes and she laughed as she had not in years. The Queen rode closer and spoke, a victorious smile tilting her lovely lips, "Come and mount behind me, my Janet. My horse shall bear us both." Janet shook her head mutely and held her horse's reins all the tighter. The Queen looked amused. "Give me a kiss then and ride at my side."

She reached for Janet who did not pull away. The Queen's lips burned against hers until she broke away laughing, enchanted by a glamour all her own. Then, bright and full of mortal promise, she urged her horse into a gallop and rode with into Faery with the Queen at her side.

M. Le Maupin

My cough has returned and I fear that I have another long day abed before me. Once again, Geoffrey, my scribe, sits by the window writing all the tales that I have in me about what has come before this pass that I currently find myself in. I laugh to think how shocked my erstwhile comrades would be to see me like this. Then I remember the beginning of it all...

"Aubigny! Where are you, girl?"

My mother's voice pierced the theater, even into old Monsieur Jacques' dank subterranean chamber, where he was training me in swordplay. Old Jacques lowered his épée and chuckled, "You'll catch it again, Aubigny, when she finds you in breeches. Ah well, enough for today. You must work on your guard for our next lesson."

My mother charged into the chamber with only the briefest of knocks. "Ah, mon dieu! Monsieur Jacques, you are turning my daughter into a boy!" I glanced down at my leather doublet, boots, breeches and sword and had to agree that there was a stunning resemblance.

"But, Mamá," I responded, "Monsieur de La Salle says that I play a magnificent young man and that such deception is all the rage in Paris now! Besides, my voice is too deep and I am too lean to play the ingénues."

"M. La Salle is a barbarian, with no hint of propriety! Come to my room for your fitting, if you please, mademoiselle." I bowed to Jacques, and sheathed my sword, following my mother forth with a deep sigh. We ascended the steep, dusty stairs of the Lyons Opera Theater to our room, where she worked making costumes for us, and for the other actors who could afford to pay her.

"How do you expect to find a husband or even a lover dressed in such a fashion, Aubigny?" Mamá began her standard tirade. "When I was the friend of Monsieur le Comte de Argonne, I was always most feminine and refined. That is what such men of quality are drawn to."

M. le Comte was occasionally rumored about the Opera to be my absent father, a piece of gossip which my mother had declined to confirm. In any case, when le Comte and Mamá ceased to be "friends," he helped her to obtain a position as a minor player in the Opera de Lyons, thereby returning her to whence they met.

As a result, I grew up in the theater, playing pageboys and children's roles when I was small, then graduating to my current status as I aged. At seventeen, I was lean and strong, lacking in significant feminine curves and possessed of an aquiline nose. Consequently I was much too fierce in appearance to sing the roles of young maidens longing for love and rescue.

I responded by learning early in life that women's clothes and women's lives were both uncomfortable and confining. As a result, there was no place for a woman such as myself outside the Opera in this France in the year of Our Lord 1690.

My mother daily and loudly despaired of marrying me off, or at least acquiring a rich gentleman protector for me. With this in mind, M. la Salle, the Opera director, with an eye to his purse, encouraged me to try the young men's roles and to learn to fence and fight so that I might at least be more believable to our audiences, perhaps even earn my own way.

Mamá emerged from the hanging costumes with a sigh that broke up my thoughts. She was carrying a blue satin waistcoat, a silk shirt, and other parts of the costume that I would require to sing the part of Pyramus, devoted lover of Thisbe, for the coming fortnight. "Here it is. Put it on and I'll see what needs to be changed," she said, shaking her head regretfully. "I hope this folly of yours ends soon, before it's too late to find you a man."

I had little interest in men and less desire to share that information with her, so I remained silent. I wanted only to be a star of the Opera, preferably in Paris, where one could perform for the King, and to be a master swordsman, a status I could not achieve as a woman. But with neither desire likely to be fulfilled at present, my future lay in Lyons, insofar as I could see, secured by failing to share my innermost thoughts with Mamá.

Those thoughts were overcome by my nerves for the next few days, at least until the opening night of the Opera. Then, I was simply terrified. It was my first time singing a major role, and it was all I could do to go out on stage. Once there, I managed to sing mawkishly of my love to our soprano, Mademoiselle Eugenié, she of the long blonde curls and simpering looks. All the while, I forced myself to remain oblivious to the audience as well as I could.

The lovely Eugenié made that simpler by simply singing, rather than flirting the way she normally did. Being pretty and empty-headed, but possessed of a sweet voice, she played all the young women in need of rescue. Seldom did she lose the opportunity to tell me that I was such a pretty young man myself that had I been one in life, she would not have hesitated to fall in love with me. This she emphasized with coquettish looks and sighs, both on and off stage, which often made me blush.

That evening, I had no time for blushes. I concentrated fiercely on singing my best, forcing myself to remain unconscious of both her false advances and the audience. And unaware I remained until that fateful moment when I gazed about, looking for Thisbe/Eugenié under the tree where we were to meet our fates.

My glance fell inadvertently upon the audience where I saw a young mademoiselle seated with the merchants and others of their class. I had a brief glimpse of striking dark eyes and powdered hair, face upturned to gaze raptly at the stage and at me. I paused for moment, then turned to find Thisbe's bloody cloak upon the ground, trying to give the lady no more thought while I was singing. Yet I could feel my heart race whenever my gaze crept in her direction.

When the Opera ended, the performers, I among them, mingled with the wealthy patrons and those who wanted to appear to be such. I glanced around, failing to see the beauty from the audience in the crowd milling about on the stage. My heart was a rock in my breast.

But after accepting the congratulations of our local deputy, I felt a tug on my sleeve. A small, grubby boy held out a dainty kerchief, trimmed with lace.

"Here, you!" I grabbed him, "Where did this come from?"

"A mademoiselle in the crowd. I don't know her name! I didn't steal anything!" came tumbling out in response. I patted him reassuringly, and gave him a sou to send him on his way.

"An admirer, eh?" commented Jacques as he passed by.

"That will last only until she learns that I am a maid," I said, with all of the cynicism born of my seventeen years of worldly experience. Old Jacques wriggled his eyebrows in amusement and moved on to converse with a merchant as I hurriedly stuffed the cloth into my belt with only the most cursory sniff at its perfume.

For several nights thereafter, of course, I dreamt of dark eyes in a pale face. In the meantime, the Opera was well received in Lyons and there was great speculation as to my sex. I was named only as "M. le Maupin" to increase the mystery, which in its turn, kept the crowds coming back.

The attentions of the local nobles and rich merchants increased at the end of each performance; I received several offers from gentlemen who presumed me to be a boy, which I politely declined. Sodomites were common enough in both the Opera and the audience; while they did not disturb me, I had little to desire to demonstrate why I was not what they sought.

But on the third night, a folded note was pressed upon me by another small boy. Flirting as I was with several very minor nobles, I had no chance to respond or pursue. They laughed at my confusion and one attempted to pluck the note from my hand. I resisted, laughing, and swiftly concealed it until I could read it in privacy. A quick turn away to the deserted edge of the stage bought me a chance to peruse its contents a few moments later.

"Pyramus, come to the garden of the house of Montmorency, Rue de Arcadié at midnight tomorrow, or I die!" My heart raced. Could it be my mademoiselle? And if it was, what would she say upon learning that I was not a young man, as she thought? No, I could not go! It was too much to bear. And yet...I had never been in love, for I wanted no men, or at least none that I had met so far. I felt myself begin to waiver as I turned this issue over in my mind.

I found that I was drawn to the idea of this girl, for I hoped desperately that it was she. I wanted to speak with her, hoping against hope that she would not hate me for my disguise. Eugenié had her pick of admirers and I desperately wanted one of my own. Could such a thing as I pondered be possible?

I had heard the other players speak in whispers of unspeakable acts committed in convents. I thought longingly of what I understood of such stories, though I was terribly lacking in details. Oh, but what I would have given to find out! I suspected those tales might be the answer to my dilemma, but since I had no way to find out at present, I must seize the chance. At that moment, my mind was made up. I found that I wanted to live and love as if I were the man that many thought I was.

Such thoughts filled my time until the next performance, which I stumbled through, far from my best. I fled the wrath of M. la Salle into the belly of the Opera House. In our room, I found my sturdy leather doublet, a cloak, boots and the rest of the costume that I needed to play the role I wanted to essay. I washed the powder from my face, and found a more serviceable wig and hat. My épée was in the corner and I snatched it up as I ran out, daring to live as a man for a few fleeting hours.

The cobbled streets were quiet and dark, illuminated only by the moon and occasional torchlight, as I moved swiftly toward my destination. I was careful, hunting the shadows for thieves and others as I went. Perhaps it was my newly found hot blood that gave me such courage, but since I knew that most would see me as a somewhat impoverished youth, I feared only robbery.

I reached the house at last, without incident. The garden had a high stone wall that ran the length of the house, marking it as that of a wealthy family. The house of Montmorency were wool merchants according to the gossip I had heard, there being little enough said of them apart from that. The iron gate that led to the garden was unlocked and slightly ajar; I could see no lamps burning in the windows of the house.

A weary looking maid, somewhat stooped from age, met me in the deserted garden. She studied me sharply, then stated in crisp, disapproving tones, "My mistress bids you wait until she comes."

I bowed in acknowledgment. An eternity passed before I heard the muted rustle of a skirt brushing against the shrubbery. By the light of the moon, I saw my lady from the Opera, and she was passing fair, to borrow a phrase from my much-loved ballads.

"Pyramus, you came," she whispered as she drew near, the maid hovering anxiously nearby as a chaperone. My heart raced as I removed my hat and bowed. "Oh, you are as handsome close up as you are on the stage," she murmured as I stood. She was plump, with her hair done a la mode and carefully powdered to ape the nobility. It accented her striking features and lovely dark eyes. She seemed no more than sixteen summers.

She gazed coquettishly at me from under her long dark lashes, "Come and sit in the arbor with me. Then no one can see us from the house." Her name was Amelié, and as I learned during our talk in the arbor, she was betrothed to a Monsieur de Guise, scion of another local merchant house. She confessed that she had made a small wager with her friends that she would dare to have a chaperoned rendezvous with the beautiful young man from the Opera. My heart sank, as she chatted on, more at ease because I was such a "gentleman."

To cover my dismay, I seized her hand and quoted a love poem that a hapless young singer had once spoken to me in a futile effort to warm my heart. She paused before my passion, moist lips quivering in the moonlight. I longed to kiss her, a desire I had never known before. The maid hovered nervously, "My lady, we must go inside before you are discovered."

Amelié pressed my hand, and I swiftly pulled her delicate fingers to my lips, placing on them the heated kiss that I wished to give her mouth. "Come back tomorrow!" she said, gazing longingly at me.

The maid tugged her up the path to the house. My feet had wings as I left the garden and returned to the rooms that I shared with Mamá, and I dreamt of nothing but her that night.

I went the next night and the night after to the garden, giving no thought to the future, to her betrothal, or to my deception. I dared to think that she gazed upon me with affection, as on the third night, she favored me with a lock of her hair. I pressed it to my lips and placed it in my pouch.

Her face filled my days and nights both with dreams and visions that I knew to be impossible. For what could I say? "Come, we will be spinster milk maids together?" Such nonsense.

The days passed, and Pyramus and the ever insipid Thisbe died beautifully and tragically, night after night. M. la Salle said that he had never seen such pathos in me before, such depth of feeling. Old Jacques merely winked and wriggled his eyebrows, while Mamá was consumed with curiosity. "Where do you go so late at night, ma cherié? Have you found a friend? Is he of noble birth?"

In my head, I knew that I had heard too many ballads and that such a love could never be, but my heart was heedless. I hesitated to tell my beloved of my true nature, knowing that such a revelation would end our trysts. I hardly knew what I wanted, save only to kiss her and hear her sweet voice.

But I hoped on. Our love would be chaste and pure and she would never find out that I was a woman. Or perhaps, she would find out, and love me despite my deception. Such was the stuff of my daydreams.

At the same time, the man's role that I had adopted became ever more comfortable to me. It became harder and harder to don skirts and other confining women's clothes. I took to wearing leather bands on my wrists to strengthen them for sword practice. This also had the added advantage of concealing their relative narrowness. In truth, I wanted the advantages that came with manhood, such as the not inconsiderable benefit of wearing bearable garments and the chance to court my love. Oh, to have been born a man!

Since I was not, I spent many tormented hours pondering how to reveal myself to my love. My Amelié was a romantic girl who, as far as I knew, saw me as a pretty young man, sensitive far above the norm. She was intelligent, as well as beautiful, and had something of a convent education, but that alone gave me no hint as to how she would take my revelation.

But I sensed that she had begun to reciprocate my affections, and dared to hope that she loved me as I loved her. Even as I hoped for such a thing, it terrified me. There was still the small matter of my deception, not to mention her affianced husband to deal with.

Inevitably, the night came when I resolved to live with the lie no more. I must tell her that I was, in fact, a woman. I knew it to be the honorable thing to do, even if it ended my greatest happiness. I still hoped otherwise. But there was no longer any comfort to be found in falsehood, as it did not suit me. I thought that, perhaps, if she spurned me, as spurn me she probably would, I would go to Paris to try my fortune in the Opera there.

And so, with a heavy heart and lagging steps, I returned to the garden at the usual time, armed as usual to deter assaults. But this time, as I entered the garden, I sensed something amiss. An unknown hand slammed the gate behind me as I entered.

"So! This is the stripling who would make a fool of me," a deep male voice growled. I turned sharply to find myself facing a large, ill-favored man, older than myself and far drunker. "I should run you through as you stand there, boy. But I'll not be called a murderer for aught. Draw that sword, and we'll see what you're made of."

This could be none other than M. de Guise, my rival for Amelié's love. My blood boiled that he should have what I could not. My épée was in my hand before I knew what I was about. "En garde, monsieur! I will fight you for my lady's love."

He laughed, a harsh, angry sound, and drew his sword as well.

Our blades clashed, neither of us giving thought to our surroundings or that such combat would wake the house. He was more practiced with the blade, but the drink slowed him down. I thought of Jacques' teachings as we circled. Thrust, parry, thrust again. I leapt backward, narrowly avoiding a vicious swipe. This man meant to kill me, and I had no good idea of whether I could slay him. Fear filled me as he drove me back, and back again, our blades glinting in the moonlight.

I employed a trick that Jacques had taught me and feinted low, then slashed his arm as he lunged. First blood was mine. Now, I was more determined. My courage grew. I cut him again as we circled. He bled freely and his lunges became more desperate.

At last, I heard shouts from the household and the distant footsteps of the night watch. I had to make my escape or face the penalty for dueling against the King's law. I feinted once more, then lunged. Success was mine and my blade pierced his breast. He fell, and I fled out the garden gate, servants pouring from the house behind me.

As I ran through the cobbled streets, I could hear the heavy steps of pursuers behind me. I darted to the right up an alley, and turned left at the next, then right again up into a maze of alleys. Soon I was in a part of the city that I had never seen before, having had no earlier need to know aught of alleyways or of escaping from the watch. I paused to wipe my rival's blood from my blade and sheath it. In my haste, I had run off with my sword in my hand.

I could no longer hear my pursuers so I slumped against the alley wall to take stock of my surroundings. I was filled with a mixture of exaltation and horror: had I killed my rival? I had proven myself capable of handling a sword, but if I had murdered my love's fiancé, there would be a price upon my head and I would have to flee France. The sight of blood did not horrify me, in part because it seemed so unreal, but the thought of having possibly murdered my rival stunned me. Fear brought me back to the present with a start.

Under my current circumstances, I realized I could not afford to dwell on these thoughts, but must find a way back to the Opera while evading all who might capture me. I looked about me. The neighborhood seemed to be a poor one, the streets lined with shabby homes and shops, and more rats and sewage than even I was accustomed to sharing the alleyway with me.

My sense of the direction of my flight was not clear, but it seemed to me that I had fled south and east from the garden and that the theater lay somewhere to my left. I needed to be on my way before I was set upon by one of the gangs of ruffians who frequented such areas. This thought lent wings to my heels, as I set off in what I believed was the correct direction.

I skulked through a seemingly deserted alleyway to enter upon a slightly broader street. At that moment afire as I was with terror, I thought I heard a woman's faint cry coming from somewhere nearby. My feet moved me forward before I'd a chance to think on the dangers of my situation, my épée singing from its scabbard as I drew it. I came upon a grisly scene as I rounded the corner: two men, one holding the arms of an elderly dame while the other pawed through her battered basket and growled threats at her.

"Begone scum! You'll not get your sport this night!" I cried as I ran forward. The one I approached directly dropped the dame's basket and drew his knife, snarling wordlessly. I batted it aside, my strength growing with my anger. "Must I slay you to defend this old woman?" I shouted.

"Not me," muttered the second rowdy, as he released her and ran off into the shadows. The remaining bully, seeing that he had been deserted, and that my sword outmatched his knife, also chose to take his leave precipitously. I watched him scramble awkwardly out of sight.

The dame had retrieved her possessions when I looked back, and dropped a small curtsey to me, "Mercí, young Monsieur. You are very kind to rescue a humble peasant."

"I'm not far above you in station, Madam. I am but a humble player, at your service." I bowed.

She gazed at me sharply. "And what brings such a fine young man to the alleys of Lyons after midnight?" she inquired.

"It is a long tale. In part I am here because I lost my way. May I escort you to your home?" I responded.

"That loss of your way wouldn't have occurred while fleeing the watch, would it?"

I faltered before her sharp eyes and amused, but wary smile. "I swear I mean you no harm," I stammered.

"Oh, I know that. Yes, I think it would be for the best if you came with me." With that, she hooked her arm through mine, once I had sheathed my blade again, and we continued briskly down the street.

"And what brings a lady of your years onto the streets at such an hour?" I ventured.

She laughed drily. "I've been attending a late birthing. I'm the midwife for this part of the city."

We soon reached a house in somewhat better repair than those around it; flowers grew in window boxes, and the old doorstep was well swept. "Lad, does the watch know who you are and where you live?" she inquired, gazing sharply up at me.

I faltered; surely my Amelié would not betray me. Yet her maid might be induced to talk. They would search the Opera for me! I had nowhere to go. The shock must have shown on my face. The old dame caught my arm, "Come inside and sit a bit, young one, before you think on what to do next."

I followed her inside in a daze. The house was poor, but clean, with sparse furniture, and filled with the hubbub of several cats emerging to greet their mistress. I heard the clatter of another occupant, recently disturbed from her rest. A slightly younger woman than the one I had rescued, clad only in her nightclothes, burst through a doorway, "Louise, where have you been? Oh! Who have you brought to our house?" She pressed a hand up to her breast in shock as she stared at me.

"The young Monsieur rescued me from some bravos on the street. He needs a place to rest, and my guess is also a bite to eat." She gazed shrewdly at me, as she barred the door and lit a second lamp. She looked more closely at me, "Or should I say, 'Mademoiselle'?"

I had been unmasked, and on such short acquaintance! Visions of returning to the life of a homely maid, cast out of the Opera and executed for my crime filled my mind. I gave her a stricken look. “There, there,” she said, patting my arm, “I’ve seen your like before, that’s all.”

“My like?” I stammered.

“Females who live best as men. Do you also prefer the company of women?” she inquired.

“I do not rightly know what you mean,” I blurted, stunned by such a question.

“Oh Louise! You’re shocking her!” the younger woman cried, “Come, sit by the fire. There’s some soup left from the evening meal. I’ll fetch it.” With that she bustled out of the room.

I sat on the bench she had pushed me onto, my brain reeling. “What do you mean by that question?” I demanded.

Louise seated herself on the opposite bench. “Is a young lady the cause of your flight?”

I buried my head in my hands. “She does not know my true nature! I fought a duel with her fiancé and may have killed him in her very garden! I can never see her again! And I cannot return to the Opera,” I sobbed.

“Ah my child, there are always ways,” she said knowingly, giving my shoulder a soothing pat. The younger woman, whose name I soon learned, was Anne, reappeared with soup in a sturdy earthenware bowl. They urged me to eat, though I’d no stomach for it. I forced myself to oblige to show gratitude for their hospitality.

As I ate in lackluster fashion, they told me an astonishing tale. Anne had been a serving wench in a bordello on the other side of the city. The house had often called upon Louise to provide herbs “to curb the curse of Eve,” as she put it, though I had little idea of what she meant. I knew that many of the actresses at the Opera took concoctions to ensure that they would not be with child, and unable to perform, so I assumed she referred to these.

I was ashamed to admit my ignorance and the tale flowed on without me.

Apparently, Louise had met Anne on her frequent visits to the place, and love had flourished between them. They elected to establish their home away from the bordello, with Anne serving as Louise's assistant, and had lived thus together quite happily for some years. Such an idea had never occurred to me, even in my wildest dreams. That two women could be companions! This notion gave me a brief rosy vision of my Amelié and myself, settling in a similar way.

This lasted until I remembered that neither of us knew aught of healing or herbs. Moreover, Amelié did not even know the true nature of the object of her affections. As I mulled this over, the excesses of the evening suddenly took their toll. Louise and Anne removed my sword and outer garments as I stood in an exhausted stupor, then they placed me on a straw pallet on the floor where I fell immediately asleep.

When I awoke next morning, I was completely disoriented by my new strange quarters. Anne was baking black bread upon the hearth, while Louise bustled about gathering bundles of dried herbs from different corners of the room. "Ah you're awake! Well, sit up and have some bread." I sat, discovering that my new life as daring young hero took a great toll in aches and pains. But I was young, and some bread and gruel soon brought me around. And back to the difficulty of my circumstances, but Louise allowed no time for brooding.

"All right, young one, we've some clothes of Anne's brother that he has no more need of, in the cupboard there. Put them on and help me take these herbs to the apothecary's. We'll tell them that you're Anne's brother, come to stay a few days." I obediently wandered over to the cupboard, and dressed myself in the aforementioned clothes, threadbare tradesman's garb that was too long in the legs and too broad in the shoulders. Nevertheless, I tucked and folded until I could trail Louise out onto the street to carry her bundles without being a three-day wonder.

Several days passed in a bewildered blur as I pondered my fortune and Anne and Louise kindly took care of me until I regained my spirits. I realized that there was nothing for it but to leave Lyons and go to Paris. For there was always the Opera and I had not yet abandoned my dreams.

My youthful foolishness ensured that I resolved to bid my adieus to Mamá and to Amelié before I departed, despite the risks. This resolve I shared with my new friends, and they made every effort to dissuade me. When they failed, Anne kindly gave me her brother's garb as a disguise. "He's long gone, he'll not be needing it," she said. "Be careful," and lightly kissed my cheek.

"How can I repay you?" I asked.

"Repay the kindness to another in need," Louise said, "and don't be believing none of that nonsense about old women and witchcraft."

I took my leave, pondering her advice in some confusion. What did witches have to do with my circumstances? I wondered as I walked purposefully toward our rooms, my cavalier's clothing and épée carefully bundled up in a large package under my arm.

As I got closer, I became more cautious, but saw no sign of the watch, nor perhaps more fortunately, anyone from the Opera who might have seen through my disguise. Mamá herself scarcely recognized me when I knocked, pausing for a moment, then flinging her arms around me with a great shriek.

"Ma cherié! Where have you been? I thought you were done for!" She and Jacques had convinced the watch that the young actor who had played Pyramus had fled the city upon the night of the assault on M. de Guise. He had survived the duel and was on the mend, but it was plain that I could not continue singing in the Opera Lyons.

"Here is your pay, my love. M. le Comte has provided a letter of introduction to a friend of his in Paris, the Abbe Condé at the Church of Ste. Bartolomé, who may be able to help you." She assisted me in bundling up my clothing, with some bread and cheese for the journey.

I explained that I had one errand to run in my maid's clothes. She eyed me sharply, "I suppose it has to do with your late nights and the reason that the watch is hunting for you?" I nodded. "Oh, you're sure to get yourself murdered at this rate," she wrung her hands despairingly. "Very well, go to your death. There is nothing your heartbroken mother can say to stop you."

Transformed once more into a maid, I walked the streets to the Rue de Arcadié. I came to the kitchen gate and asked to speak to Amelié, on the pretence that I came on an errand from the dressmaker's. Though I shook with terror and anticipation, I had to bid my love farewell. I forced myself to remain until a maid ushered me into the deserted main room.

Amelié entered looking haggard and worn, "Yes? What is it?" I pulled a locket from my bodice, and without a word, showed her the lock of hair within. "You know where he is!" she hissed in a fierce whisper, catching my arm, "Tell me!" I pulled the maid's cap from my head and looked into her eyes.

She studied me avidly, hand pressed to her mouth. Her eyes widened with recognition and she took a step back. I turned to go, that single look of shock burning a hole in my heart. "Wait!" she whispered again. "I'm to be sent to a convent because of you! M. le Guise said he'll not have a wife who is not pure, and my father wants to hide me away until the scandal dies away. And now this!" She glared fiercely at me. "Just what do you plan to do?" she studied me through narrowed dark eyes, "You are a maid in truth, are you not?"

"Aye. I am going to Paris to make my way there," I said softly, bracing for yet more rejection, but puzzled by her reaction. It was far different from what I feared. She turned from me, hands clasping and unclasping with emotion.

"Not without me, you're not!" she spun back around to face me.

I staggered in shock. "If I stay, I'll be married off to some old man who can't buy himself another young wife. Or I'll be locked up in that convent, reciting interminable prayers until I die," she paced, wringing her hands as she walked. "You must get me some peasant maid's clothes, like to those you are wearing. I suppose you're going as a man?" I nodded. "It's as well. I can claim you as husband or brother as need arises, and 'tis plain that you're good in a brawl. You should certainly be able to protect me. Now you must go before they become suspicious. Do close your mouth. You look like a fish."

"I love you," I blurted. Her face, hardened in determination, softened as she gazed on me.

"You must, to have come back to see me," she said and smiled gently for the first time since I entered. "But I must go. This afternoon, my maid and I go to the dressmaker's, for I go to the convent not three days hence, and my father wants my garb appropriately somber. You must follow and distract my maid long enough for me to slip away. I will find you and we will leave the city together."

My heart was full to bursting as I left. Headstrong I knew my love to be, but to show such daring! The strength of my passion increased with each step.

I returned to bid my lengthy adieus to Mamá, who was suspicious as usual, and wailed her lamentations until my departure, dressed once more as a cavalier. "I hope she's worth the risk," she said as she arranged my shirt and surcoat. "I'm not blind or foolish," she added to my stunned face. She kissed me, told me to send her messages assuring her of my safety, then sent me forth. I went, convinced that my life and all my intentions were a sort of broadsheet apparent to all passersby.

An age passed before my love came forth, heavily cloaked and accompanied by her maid. I followed them until I felt the crowd had grown sufficient to hide her flight. I contrived to bump into her maid in a manner which seemed both irritating and suspicious. She whirled to face me as I lurched drunkenly out of range of her outstretched arm.

"Here, you drunken sot! What are you doing, crashing into a respectable woman like me?" The crowd's attention focused upon us as I slurred drunken apologies and attempted to stagger up a side street. She continued to call imprecations at me as I moved away, finally turning to realize that her lady was no longer there. I slunk up an alleyway, as she cried out, "My lady! She's been stolen! Call the watch!"

I stayed where I was, slumped against a stone wall, coated in I knew not what substances and tried to look drunk. "Come on!" A small cloaked figure darted into the alley, "She'll have the watch on us!" We emerged after she removed her cloak, and substituted the one I had brought. Then we walked slowly, arm in arm, up the cobbled street toward the city gate.

***

I yawned, my thoughts lost in the past and Geoffrey stood and began to quietly pack his things. Tomorrow, perhaps, I would tell him of our adventures in Paris and how I came to the Court. There would be time enough.

Spell, Book and Candle

Mom always told me to stay away from the love spells. She would know; she and Dad tried them all, back in their "Let's stay together for the children" phase. We had the therapy bills to prove it. So I resolved early on to learn from their mistakes and get my dates the traditional way. Most of the time.

That didn't apply to selling the tools to others, however. Love and lust are big sellers here at Lovejoy's Magical Books and Mystical Goods Emporium. You name the spell workings and we sell it. Still, I usually left my work at work and sent the crazy stuff out the door with the herbs, the candles and the little books in the customers' shopping bags. It wasn't like they could do much harm with them. Or at least that was store policy until Mona Santiago stopped by.

Mona and I had history, provided 'history' refers to major dyke drama. I dumped her in college for some sweet young thing who seemed like less work. After that, Mona made it her mission to break up every college relationship I had. It got to be a game. I'd pick up girls just to see how long it would take her to steal or drive them away.

We feuded right up until graduation, then went our separate ways, her to the big city life of corporate magic she'd always dreamed of, me to run the family business in the burbs. We hadn't done more than exchange the occasional email in six or seven years. Except, of course, for those dreams I had about her almost every night.

Even so, I'd forgotten just how...compelling she was in person. Especially when she was standing in front of me in my own little shop. That gorgeous face with those huge dark eyes, the most kissable lips I'd ever seen, that spectacular body. I made myself stop inventorying and plastered on a nonchalant welcoming smile that fooled no one.

"Selena, honey! It's been ages!" Mona lunged around the counter and clutched me to her curves in a way that made me feel more than friendly. She followed it up with a kiss on the lips, which was good, except it was the kind you give your ex: no tongue and less passion.

Not the kind of reunion I'd hoped for, alas. I bit back a sigh. I hadn't dated in months and Mona was looking better than good. But then, she always did. I made my lips form words. "What brings you out to the burbs? Need some candles for that thriving corporate Santeria practice of yours?"

"Sweetie, that's old school." Mona gave me a blinding smile. "I use circuits and wires for the work stuff now, not candles. But you have some things I do need." She looked around and wrinkled her nose at the stuff piled on the shelves. And hanging off the shelves. And sitting on the floor. Hey, at least I knew where everything was.

This visit was beginning to depress me so I switched modes, "Then what can I help the corporate director with today?" With any luck, she'd buy enough of the special books in the back to pay my property taxes this year. After all, hot is hot but business is business.

"Still your repressed New England shop keeper self, I see." Mona wrinkled the perfect cocoa butter skin on her almost equally perfect nose. Someone had clearly had some work done since college.

I couldn't help but notice her lack of shared enthusiasm about my current look. Maybe it was time to be less repressed. "Not all of us can handle those cool corporate jobs. But since you're out here in the sticks anyway, how about I show you the books in the back and maybe take you to dinner for old time's sake?" I leered hopefully and managed, just barely, not to bat my eyelashes.

For an instant, it looked like she was reminiscing about the good old days. Then, as if oblivious to smacking down one of my favorite fantasies, she shook her head, spilling glorious jet-black locks over her shoulders with abandon. "I'm sorry, Selena. Sometime soon, I promise. I have to get back tonight for work. And I still need this stuff." She pulled a list out of her bag and dropped it on the counter.

I looked down as I picked it up so that she wouldn't see how much I wanted to plead with her about going out with me tonight. At that moment that I realized how bad I still had it. I wondered if she felt even a ghost of all that college passion. Some crazy part of me parted my lips to ask.

"You can see what I want it for. I mean it seems nuts, right, me trying to use a love spell to get someone infatuated with me? But it's only a little one, just enough to give her a crush on me. I can do the rest but I need a way in." Mona leaned against the counter and stared dreamily past me like I was part of the wall.

I cringed inside and made myself read the list. Red candles, the ultimate love spell cliché. The usual herbs: Dragon's Reed, lavender, laurel and some other miscellaneous leafy greens with a kick. Then the title of the first book caught my eye: *Making Them Your Own* by Owen Lovejoy. Dear old Dad's first book, the one where he explored using love spells for manipulation and control. I shuddered. Maybe she didn't know what she was asking for. "You sure you want this book? I've got a lot better titles."

She had the good sense to look very contrite; it suited her. "Oh hon, I'm sorry! I know how you feel about your dad and all that mess between him and your mom when you were growing up. I didn't mean to be so thoughtless. I can get it somewhere else if you'd rather; I just figured you'd have it. And could use the business." This time she frowned at my poor shelves and they sank under her stare.

"Hey! Stop torturing my furniture!" I was frowning now too and Mona had the good grace to look guilty. "At least tell me why you're doing this. You, of all people, should have women eating out of your hand without using magic."

"I'm in love and she likes me, I know she does. But I can't tell how she likes me. My regular magic doesn't seem to work on her. I'm starting to worry that she might be…straight." Mona blushed scarlet and stared down at the carpet, then looked up defiantly. "But she'll be hot for me within in the week once I work this spell."

I was horrified; this kind of stuff always ended badly for everyone involved. It was at that moment that my duty became clear. I had to save Mona from herself and I had to do it soon. Plans galloped into and out of my brain. I dismissed several at lightning speed until I got to the last one. I could do what I'd wanted to do since college and make Mona fall in love with me again, just for a little while until this infatuation wore off. Once that notion took root, I was like a missile pointed at a target.

I walked out from behind the counter over to the shelves without meeting Mona's eyes. She had a gift for seeing the truth and I was guessing that my expression wouldn't look very honest. "Just hang out for a minute. I know where everything is – I'll bring it all out," I called over one shoulder.

Then I made a mad dash for the shelves in the back. I kept the serious stuff there and given Mona's powers, I was going to need everything I could find. I got the stuff from her list as I went, leaving the herbs and the books I needed until last. My Book of Shadows came easily from its hiding place and I greeted it like an old friend. It had been far too long since I'd done any real magic.

I found Dad's book on the darkest bookcase on the bottom shelf. This was where I kept that stuff that actually worked, even for novices, mostly because it had unintended consequences. The tourists never made it back here; a simple 'Don't Notice Me' kept them out of trouble. But then trouble was my business, more or less. And I was about to have plenty of it.

I headed back out to the counter. "I've got everything. Had to grab a few more things for a mail order while I was at it." I gave Mona my cheeriest smile.

She frowned suspiciously. "Aren't you going to say anything more about what I said?"

"Like what? Chasing het girls is a bad idea? You know that. Using love spells on the wrong person isn't that great of an idea either? Think you've got that one down too. What more can I add?" I bared my teeth in something like a smile.

"I dunno. Maybe 'Why is this one so special, Mona'?"

Great. She wanted to talk and I just wanted to bewitch her back to our red-hot salad days. I found myself momentarily distracted by a vision of what she looked like when she was wearing a lot less than she had on now. She must have read my mind since she scowled at me long enough to bring on wrinkles. "I guess I don't want to know right now." I mumbled.

She looked apologetic, then shrugged. A few moments later, money had changed hands and I was watching her perfect butt swing its way out the door. If I were a TV witch, this would be the point where my chatty familiar would give me sound advice, which I would then ignore. But then, if I were a TV witch, I wouldn't be a dyke with the hots for her old college sweetie. Not to mention the fact that my familiar, Pyewacket, never said much except 'Meow.'

I pulled my Book of Shadows from my back pocket and flipped through its stained and dog-eared pages to some notes that I remembered making a few years back. Ah, there it was: Rekindling Lost Loves. There was the light and fluffy version, all scents and candles and romantic dinners. Then there was the one I adapted from Dad's original, with a few extras from other sources. I'd never had the nerve to try it before but this situation called for something extra.

Whatever rational parts of my brain that I had left were making unhappy whimpering sounds right about then. I overruled them. I had enough control now that I could make this work without permanent damage or side effects. I was sure of that. I hoped. In any case, I could always call it back and what I was doing was no worse than what Mona was planning. At least I was doing it to someone who I knew for sure liked girls.

I concentrated on that thought while I read my notes, dismissing the last of my guilt pangs. The spell wasn't as complete as I remembered it being and my notes pointed me to another book. I found myself staring at the cover of *Spells and Enchantments* by Lady Isabelle Hubert as it sat there in all of its crumbling leather splendor. I couldn't shake the sense that the tome was looking back at me.

I made myself touch the cover. For a book with such an innocuous title, it had the worst magical feel of any book I kept in the store. Lady Isabelle was an ancestor of mine and family history claimed that Lady Isabelle had narrowly avoided the stake, back in the seventeenth century. The witch finders had lost much of their clout by then anyway, but the fact of the matter was that Isabelle had a way of seeming to be someone else whenever there was a problem. She lived to a ripe old age, using her powers to get whatever she wanted well past her hundredth birthday.

One thing that Isabelle liked was reliable companionship. She was a woman ahead of her time so gender was less important than susceptibility to her magic. There were one or two grim little stories about her taking over her lovers' bodies, but I wasn't after those spells. No, what Isabelle had to offer was love spells possessed of great speed and effectiveness. Anything else I had would take months to reel in my prey but one of hers would take no more than a few hours.

I flipped her book open and paged through until I could read the words in Lady Isabelle's flowing script in several languages: *Finding and Holding Love*. She wasn't big on titles. I looked over the wording: calling on Hecate and Aphrodite, calling on various demons, blah, blah, herbs, something of the beloved's, something of yours. Mostly the usual stuff, with a few exceptions. One was the added line: "Let the one who belonged to me once be mine forevermore until death or I release them." The other was a few lines in some language I'd never learned; I decided they must be footnotes since they didn't seem to be part of the ritual itself.

In a more lucid frame of mind, the whole "until Death do us part or else" thing always gave me the shivers. Anything could happen with that in a casting. Sometimes the person you used it on decided to take death as an out the minute your control slipped. Sometimes the witch got too power hungry and did things to the object of the enchantment just because she or he could get away with them.

Then there was my own internal moral compass. Despite Mom and Dad's general instability, they always brought me up to be responsible for the outcome of my spells, good and bad. Sure I wanted her now but did I want Mona to be mine forever? It wasn't a question I could answer for certain. I wondered if I could edit the spell a bit when I read it.

I checked the calendar to see which moon phase we were in. The sun had set so I went and locked the door and pulled down the shades, officially closing shop a bit early. I looked at the phone and thought about calling my parents or someone from my coven for advice. Then I looked at Mona's receipt on the counter and thought about her. After that, I called the local Chinese place for delivery instead.

An hour or two later, I gathered up the various things I needed and headed out to the little private patio in the back of the store. I drew up my pentagram in chalk and sprinkled the salt around it in a circle. Then I lit the candles at the appropriate points and did some of the other odds and ends that I usually did before I began a ritual. I made a mental checklist and looked around, feeling vaguely uneasy.

But I decided I was imagining it. Pyewacket wandered out and stretched herself over a lawn chair to watch me. I scritched her behind the ears, then I went to work on my notes and Isabelle's spell.

First of all I decided to make the language of her spell less dire. I took out the call to Hecate and opted for a lesser demon than the one she used for the original. I tweaked one or two other things and decided I was as ready as I was going to get. Then I recited the spell aloud, Mona's face hovering before me as I changed the last line to "Let the one who once belonged to me renounce the one she now desires and turn to me instead for the next three months or until I release her."

There. It was official. I was now the wimpiest practitioner of the dark arts in the entire metro area, but at least the spell wasn't quite as awful as the original. Even so, there was a cold wave of power that washed its way through me when I was done, followed by a flash of heat that made me sweat. It surged over me, then out into the world toward its intended target. The sensation of raw power was disconcertingly wonderful. I closed my eyes for a minute to savor it, which lasted until Pyewacket started howling.

I looked at my normally imperturbable black cat as she shook her head and raced around the patio. Her ears were flat and her fur was standing on end from one end of her plump body to the other. I lowered my hands and blessed the circle to end the ritual. Then I tried to call her to me but she went to ground in the farthest, darkest corner of the yard.

Her eyes had an odd blue gleam in them when I followed her over. Her expression was starting to freak me out so I left her alone to go back into the store and turn the patio lights on. At least I'd be able to see what was wrong with her then. The phone rang just as I hit the switch and I reached over and picked it up automatically.

Mona's voice hit my ear like a gentle sigh. "Oh good, you're still there! Listen, I've been thinking. I need to stop by and talk to you about that spell again."

I smiled at the empty shop. Nothing like that old black magic, courtesy of Lady Isabelle. "Of course, hon. Come on over." The phone clicked off like Mona couldn't wait to be at my side and I hung up the receiver with a huge grin. This time, I wouldn't give her up for some twit. No, I was all grown up now and I knew what I wanted. She was the one and we would grow old together, scaring the neighborhood kids from the porch of our rambling Victorian.

I heard a growl from the patio and remembered Pye with a guilty start. I dashed outside to see what was still bugging her. Now, instead of hiding out in the corner, she was up on the table, staring down at Lady Isabelle's book for all the world like she was reading it. She was even wearing what looked like a little kitty frown of concentration and she was warbling some little cat song at it. I laughed as I shut the book and tucked it away in the store, along with the rest of my paraphernalia. Mona didn't need to know what I'd been up to.

Then I came back out to give Pye an ear scratch and her eyes slitted in pleasure. Her fur settled down and she started to look normal again. Judging from the way she was purring, whatever had scared her was getting erased from her little brain. Nothing a few treats wouldn't completely wipe out. I walked back inside and opened up a can of Pye's favorite food.

She sauntered, rather than ran in when I called, much like a queen accepting her due. The regal air lasted until she got a whiff of what was in the bowl in front of her. She unleashed an unearthly howl of pure indignation and hissed at the food.

I gaped. "Pye, what's the matter? You love this stuff!"

There was a sharp rap on the door behind me and I jumped about a foot. Mona's face stared back at me through the glass when I looked around the shade, then unlocked the door. My heart was racing as she charged inside, almost knocking me down. She stared around, her eyes wild, her face haggard as she demanded, "Where is she? Where is my precious darling?"

I said the first intelligent thing that popped into my head. "I'm right here, love. Who else are you looking for?"

That question got answered the split second Mona and Pye spotted each other. Next thing I knew, my once and future girlfriend and my cat were wrapped in each other's arms, figuratively speaking. Mona murmured, "Is that bad witch trying to feed you icky canned cat food? You just come right home with me, snookums and I'll cook you up something delicious." She mumbled some endearments and Pye purred back at her like she was the coolest thing ever. She turned and headed for the door with my cat in her arms.

"Snookums?" Mona could barely tolerate cats; she was more of a purse dog kind of gal. Something was clearly very wrong. I stepped in front of them. "What the hell do you think you're doing? You are not walking out of here with my cat. Besides it's me you're supposed to want."

Pye turned her face so her ears framed Mona's eyes and her head blocked out the rest, just like Kim Novak in the old movie. Mona's expression was completely blissed out but Pye gave me a look of purely malevolent intelligence. For an instant, her eyes were blue, not green. I stumbled backward in shock, catching myself on the doorframe as Mona and the cat swept out of my shop and into the night.

My heart was still racing and my legs shook as I watched them climb into Mona's sporty little car and drive off. I had to do something and fast. What had I called up that had taken over my cat? And what did it intend to do with Mona? I forced myself into action as the taillights disappeared and pulled out the books that I had hidden away behind the counter and spread them out in front of me: Book of Shadows, Isabelle's book and Dad's book: the answer was in here somewhere.

I flipped Isabelle's book open and almost screamed when it opened to the print of her face, just after the title. There was something so fierce in that face, something distinctly…feline that I couldn't help but recognize it. A ghastly realization shook me. I'd brought Isabelle back somehow, and stuck her inside Pyewacket. How the hell had I done that?

I paged quickly through to the spell and read it again. Nothing registered the first time. But the second time through I looked at the line I didn't understand. This time I recited a charm to translate it. The words flowed across the page: "Let the recitation of this spell by one of power call me back from wherever I am that I may resume my mortal span of years as I have enjoyed them ere now." Okay, I got the calling back part down but how was she planning on resuming much of anything? It wasn't too clear until I remembered the other story. Lady Izzy was some sort of body snatcher. And I had just put my cat and my ex-girlfriend in her clutches.

I needed help and I needed it right away. Dad's book practically wiggled for my attention until I gritted my teeth and opened it up at what I thought was random. The chapter title made me cringe: *Consequences and Quandaries -The Aftermath of Love Spells*. "All right, Dad. You've made your point," I growled down at the page. I nearly tossed it onto the nearest shelf but somehow, my hand wasn't cooperating. Instead, I started reading.

By dawn, I had read my way through Dad's words of wisdom and everything I could find on our family history. I drank my fourth copy of coffee and packed the things I was going to need. This time I went for the charm bags, the oils and one or two other things. For one thing, Lady Izzy needed a new shell and I wasn't volunteering so that meant bringing along the best spirit holding receptacle I could find.

Then I went out, got into my battered little Corolla and headed for Mona's condo. This time, I knew what I was getting myself into. She'd probably never talk to me again once she figured all of this out, but at least she'd be okay. The thought gave me a sharp pang in the vicinity of my heart but it was too late to worry about that now. I'd put things right, then worry about the rest later. Maybe there was a 'Making friends with your ex after you screwed up' spell floating around somewhere.

The drive was much shorter than I remembered it being, probably because hardly anyone was out and about yet. I buzzed downstairs and didn't get an answer so I spoke a minor cantrip into the security lock and walked in. The elevator was mysteriously out of order so I hiked up to the fifth floor, swearing quietly under my breath. Someone knew I was coming and it wasn't Mona.

When I got to the right floor, I was struck with the realization of how silly this all was. Clearly, I hadn't cast a spell on Mona since she wasn't in love with me so why was I here? I could just go grab breakfast at my favorite diner and open the store up early, maybe get all those mail orders done.

Uh huh. "I know what you're doing," I said to the empty air of the hallway as I waved my hands in a gesture of dismissal. For added emphasis, I whispered a spell that caused misused magic to return to its source. Something thought dark thoughts back at me, but the feeling that this was all wasted effort went away.

I walked down the no longer apparently endless hallway to Mona's door and pulled one of the charms from my bag. I fastened it to the doorknob, then used the same spell I'd used to get into the building. It didn't work this time so I broke out the angelica and the vervain, sprinkling it over the hall side of the threshold to drive back evil. Then I tried the knob again.

Mona's apartment was dark. I stumbled over and opened one of the blinds so I could see my way around, stumbled being the operative word. I wasn't sure my toes would ever recover. Once I got some light on the living room, I could see why. Mona's apartment was filled with all kinds of ottomans and cushy chairs, most of them fairly low to the floor. An elaborate scratching post tree filled one corner. It couldn't be like this all the time. This had to be Lady Izzy feeling her catnip. I wondered what else she could control Mona to do and shivered.

My quarry was nowhere to be seen so I started for one of the doors that I thought would lead to the bedroom. I uncorked a bottle of Ava Rosa for binding evil and let its scent cloud around me as I walked. Something wasn't happy but I made it across the room unscathed.

The first door turned out to be a closet so I went for the next one. Bingo. Mona was sprawled on the bed, mouth open in a gentle snore. I gave her a regretful glance before I focused on the being I had come to see.

Lady Isabelle Hubert stared back at me from Pyewacket's now completely blue eyes. She growled and hissed as she tried unsuccessfully to form words with her kitty vocal cords. I had the feeling that intent was more important than execution so whatever I was going to do, I needed to do fast. There would be no time for the candles that I usually used or any of my usual ritual.

Instead, I reached into my bag and pulled out the object that I'd brought with me from the shop. Holding Dad's book at arm's length, I started the chant, my eyes holding Isabelle's the whole time.

She shivered, then wailed in Pye's voice, a tiny cry of pain that made me falter for just an instant. Mona sat up, eyes blazing. I had always thought that was just an expression, but apparently it wasn't. I was very nearly singed. She spoke, her voice a snarl of fury, "What the hell are you doing to my cat?"

For an answer, I opened Dad's book and shouted the last few words of the entrapment spell. It was like being hit with a tornado. A sharp force slapped me against the far wall, knocking all the air out of me. I wrestled with it, trying to ignore the hideous feeling that it was working its way inside *me*. It was like struggling with an anaconda.

After the longest minutes of my life, it started to feel like something was pulling at it, drawing it away. Then the force shot past me and into the book with a hideous wail. I dropped to my knees and slammed the book shut. I shoved it into my bag. Just not before Mona was released from Lady Isabelle's hold in time to see me doing it.

She recovered fast. "What the hell did you just do? And why are you and your cat in my bedroom at the crack of dawn?" She and Pye shared a baffled stare before turning back to me.

I held out my carryall. "C'mon Pye. Let's go home." Pye jumped in without a struggle, which was an indication of how shook up she was.

"If you think you're walking out of here without an explanation, you've got…" Mona's eyes narrowed. "You did a love spell on me, didn't you? Did you make me do all that obsessive crap in college too?" Her jaw was tightening and her beautiful kissable lips were getting thin. Her hands were beginning to make gestures that I knew would probably lead to me spending the next year as furniture if I didn't get out.

"No! At least I don't think so." I was babbling when I should be fleeing. I was also reassessing my college memories and this wasn't the time. Pye chose that moment to whimper quietly and I snapped out of it. Then I bolted for the front door, running as fast as I could.

I slammed it behind me as something hard smashed into the area my head had just occupied. Then I hauled my butt down the stairs like I had wings. Hell hath no fury like the ex you emotionally jerked around because you hoped for a different outcome. I drove away, swearing off love spells for the rest of my magical existence, sure that I'd learned my lesson.

Dad's book slid a little ways out of my bag and I thought about Lady Isabelle. There had been something in the way she handled herself that I liked, now that I was almost over being terrified. I thought about her portrait and how long it had been since I'd had a girlfriend who really understood me over the screams of my common sense. Maybe one more spell, if I did it really carefully…

Red Scare

The note said that the Fat Man knew about Greta and me. It was pinned to my desk with a slick little knife, just the kind scum like his muscle would use. It was a nice touch. I could take a hint. My desk couldn't take too many more, though. A few more calling cards like this one and I'd be sitting behind a pile of matchsticks.

Personally, I didn't give a rat's ass what he knew about me. A few of my friends knew I was really a dame. So did a few of my enemies. Didn't matter much unless I was in the running for Head Gumshoe, which I wasn't. To the world, I was Dash McDermott, private dick, and whether or not I actually had one didn't seem to matter to most of my clients. Of course, that was probably because they usually had other things to worry about.

Now Greta, she was another story. She was a vid star and well on her way to being the next Femme Fatale when Lana Dean retired. A word to the Committee and she'd never work again. The Committee exists primarily to protect us from the Buggies, the Kru'ush Magir, as any right-minded citizen could tell you. Protecting us from ourselves ran a close second.

Of course, nobody outside of the Defense Forces had seen one of the Buggies since the original colonists had landed on Falcon. But we all knew that they were out there somewhere, waiting to invade and wipe us all out. Though why they hadn't for the last hundred years or so, no one could say. But as the Committee prop goes, "Preparedness is the key."

At least if you believed in bug-eyed monsters. Not me. I believed in staying away from the Committee and going to the vids every Friday like a good Revivalist. Any doubts I had about the Old Earth history they showed, I kept to myself.

Don't get me wrong. There are some great things about living here. Greta, for instance.

Thinking about her made me realize that I'd better meet the Fat Man so I clapped my homburg on my head, folded the knife and stuck it in my pocket. The office door slammed behind me as I went down the dim hallway out into the greenish-yellow sunlight.

A Packard remake cruised by, cybercell motor barely purring as the horn blared and the driver waved at Johnny, the old shoeshine guy on the corner. He waved back, then blinded me with a gold-toothed grin. "How ya doin', Mr. McDermott?"

I grinned back at him as I headed for the streetcar stop. For the thousandth time, I wondered how he paid for that dental job. Authentication like that cost more than I made in a month. He gave me a slow wink but no answers before I turned the corner.

The streetcar that showed up was called "Desire" and it was packed. Pity I just can't resist knives stuck in my desk, not even during rush hour, or I would have caught the next one. When I got off, the Casablanca's awning loomed up ahead. I sauntered down the block, resisting the urge to smooth my lapels just cause Barney the Bruiser stood outside the door watching me. I could feel my fingers ache for the handle of my raygun.

He sneered down at me as I walked up. "Why don'cha try wearing a dress for a change, ya pervert?"

"Hi Barney. Sure, I'll wear a dress for you, honey buns. Why don't you put one on too, and we'll go out for a big night at Sally's. My friends would just die to meet you."

He spat on the asphalt and I bared my teeth at him. "The Fat Boy sent me a calling card. Be a good little toady and tell him I'm here."

"You carrying heat?" A meaty paw reached for me. I stepped back.

"What do you think, sugar? That a delicate flower of womanhood like myself walks the mean streets unprotected? Fatso knows I'm not going to waste him. It'd be bad for my rep. You, on the other hand..." I looked him over speculatively. Even with the raygun on full, he'd make a hell of a pile of ashes.

He stepped back a little, muttering a string of things that I chose not to hear. I watched the big ugly vein in his forehead beat time for a minute before I pushed my way past through the red velvet curtain behind him. The space between my shoulders twitched where his little eyes were burning a hole, but I made myself act casual.

The Fat Man was sitting at his usual table by the bar, facing the door. He looked a little tired in the dim light. Kind of pasty. It cheered me up.

"What do you want, Fat Boy?" I liked messing with his title, especially since he wasn't that big, definitely not Greenstreet material. We just didn't turn out substantial rats like they did back on Earth.

He gave me an evil glare. "You like having a movie star, Mr. McDermott?" He kind of hissed the words, stopping for a long time on the "Mr." His Brit accent needed work.

"I don't think you'll get to take my place if I take a fall, Fatso. Now whaddaya want?" I stepped forward, turning slightly so I could watch Barney coming in the door and the joker standing at the bar behind the Fat Man at the same time. He probably wasn't planning on arranging any accidents for me or he wouldn't have bothered having me show up here, but hey, 'preparedness is the key.'

"Have a seat," he pointed to the chair across from him. I grabbed the one on his right instead and sat close enough that I could fry him before Barney got to me. No point in taking chances.

He pulled a face, but held up his hand to stop Barney where he was, looming a few feet away. "We found your cousin Fortune in an alley down by the Farmer's Market yesterday afternoon." He ran a descriptive finger along his wrinkled throat.

That might have brought a tear to my eye if I hadn't despised Fortune from the bottom of my heart. Aunt Mabel wouldn't be too happy, though. "Yeah? We weren't close. Whaddaya want me for?"

"Some of Fortune's friends think that I had something to do with it."

Fortune had friends? Who knew? "And?" I asked. There had to be something else. Fatso's problems were his own as far as I was concerned.

He followed up with a change of topic. "What do you know about the Kru'ush Magir, McDermott?"

"Not much. You?"

He looked like his fingers just begged to slap me. "This is big stuff. If I didn't have orders... All right. I heard that Fortune made some kind of contact with them. You know where that could lead." His voice dropped so he sounded like a vid villain.

Oh goody. I love listening to a bad Orson Welles' imitation, more than anything in the world. But critiques aside, this was out of my usual league. "Orders" on Falcon only come from the Committee but why did they care about my jackass cousin? I tried to imagine Fortune as the mastermind behind an alien invasion. It sounded kinda ambitious for a two-bit thug. "No, I don't know. Where did that "information" come from, Fatso?"

He leaned forward, looking me in the eye as hard as he could to place his insubstantial weight behind his words. "Reliable sources."

"Right. And I'm Bogart." I stood up. The Fat Man stuck a hand in his jacket. I stuck a hand in mine. Barney started moving, picking up speed as he headed in my direction, only to be stopped again by his boss' upheld hand. He glared at me as the Fat Man put a box on the table in front of me. I opened it to find a glossy goldtone pin, a big star-shaped one, the kind of shimmer that you'd get a femme if you were down on your luck but not flat broke.

"Not my style." I picked it up and flipped it over. The little red lights and the wires told me it wasn't your ordinary shimmer. But then, I never thought it was.

"It's a transmitter, better than any we can make yet. We found it on him. Our sources say it came from off-planet." I looked up at the few beads of sweat lining the fringe of what little hair he had left, then down into his tiny brown eyes. They didn't shift much. Still, I wondered why his boys were close enough to be searching the body before the Defense Forces showed up. That kind of work wasn't usually left up to the hoods, even the official ones like Fatso.

"So what do you want me to do about Fortune's taste in jewelry?"

"In light of your connections..." he steepled his little fingers together like he was thinking hard. I didn't buy it but he kept doing it anyway. "I would like to hire you on behalf of the Committee to investigate this matter. Find out if Fortune really made contact with the Buggies and what his plans were if he succeeded."

I sat back down and gave his proposal some thought. The only thing that Fortune and the Fat Man had in common was a ten-year-old turf war over the scratch trade. Supposedly my cousin was profiting from it and the Committee was out to shut it down but I had my doubts. Today's little game had to be connected to the scratch somehow. I don't know how I knew it, but I did.

The scratch, that lovely liquid silver that you slipped straight into your blood through cuts in your skin, had cost me a couple of friends. And Leandra. I looked at the Fat Man and swallowed both the sudden lump in my throat and a barely controlled desire to pull out my raygun and fry him. But Lee was long gone by now and shooting him wouldn't bring her back. Instead I decided I'd take him for everything he was worth.

"My tab's fifty credits a day. And I get my records changed," I said, almost as an afterthought. It wasn't. Femmes weren't supposed to be gumshoes, but I just wasn't Fatale material, ditto for Romantic Lead. Getting my records changed would transform me into a real gumshoe and keep the Committee off my back for the foreseeable future. Not to mention sparing me some permanent changes on a black market table that I had no desire to make.

He sputtered and jawed about the fate of our world resting in my hands and such for a few minutes. I got forty-five a day in the end and his agreement about the records. Better than I expected so I knew I wasn't expected to survive this job.

I waited till he turned to say something to Barney and I palmed the shimmer. As I left, I passed him back the closed box with his own knife, the one he had so kindly left in my desk, inside it for weight. The shimmer could come in handy, I thought, though for what I didn't know yet. Insurance, maybe.

I wandered back down the street, one baby blue peeled over my shoulder on the lookout for company. I didn't see anyone yet, but they'd be along. I hopped on the next streetcar then changed cars a couple of times on my way to the Farmer's Market just in case.

For entertainment, I tried to wrap my brain around the idea that my cousin Fortune had contacted bug-eyed monsters from outer space. My right hand toyed with the shimmer in my pocket. What kind of game was the Fat Man playing this time? From what I knew of him, there was no good reason to think that he hadn't sliced Fortune's throat himself. But I kept going anyway; it wasn't like I had anything better to do.

I got off at the Market intending to head for the alleys behind it, back where Fatso said they found Fortune. The legit farmers had their stands in the middle of the Market, piled high with "the fruits of the land," as the Committee liked to say.

I wandered over and got a porkstick. When I turned around, I caught a quick glimpse of a familiar back dodging down one of the alleys and froze. It couldn't be. Scratch junkies didn't last that long.

But I had to find out. My appetite took a quick powder, but I made myself swallow the dry meat anyway before I wound my way through the stands toward the alley. The someone I was chasing was down at the other end of the alley, walking away from me.

I nearly lost my nerve when I got a clear eyeball on her feet. They were covered in scales, almost like claws. When I looked further up, I could see something bulging under the shoulders of the blue coat. Wings? For a minute, I wondered what a Buggy really looked like; I'd always had my doubts about the Committee sparktags. Then I started down the alley after her. That was when she turned around.

It had been four years since I'd seen her last but you don't forget a femme like that. She wore a thick black veil pulled over her face, hanging down from her wide brimmed hat like a storm cloud. From what little I could see of her face, I was grateful for what it spared me. "Hey, Leandra," I spoke softly, forcing the words out.

She cringed when she saw me. I tried not do the same, tried not to remember how pretty she was back when she was my femme. Before she dumped me for Fortune and then him for the scratch. "Hello Dash." Her voice had gone all raspy, but at least she still knew me. How had she managed to change so much and still be alive? Scratch junkies never made it past the dry skin and deeper voice part. After that they just disappeared. My gut said they got iced before they got this far, but I didn't know for sure. Hell, I'd never thought about it much before.

Then I remembered Fortune. "Let's go talk, Lee. There's something I've got to tell you." Better she should hear it from me. I thought she loved Fortune before she got hooked. More than me anyway. I looked away, catching her nod from the corner of my eye. She didn't seem human any more, at least not the way I thought of us. My guts tied themselves in knots while I led the way back to the benches that ringed the outer edge of the Market.

I sat down, shaking all over. I couldn't look at her as she slithered down onto the far edge of the bench, couldn't stand listening to the sounds of things crunching and scraping that weren't the femme I loved anymore. There was a long silence before I could get the words together. "Fortune's dead, Lee." I mumbled. Now, I just wanted to get away, get sick, then drunk, then sick again to wash it out of me.

There was little sob from the other end of the bench. I handed her my handkerchief, and she grabbed it so fast I couldn't see her fingers. The rasp of scales against my fingertips made me pull away anyway, even without seeing them.

"I just saw him two nights ago. He said..." she trailed off, like she couldn't make herself go on.

I pushed, pretending that I wanted to hear more. "What?"

"That he was onto something that might make me better." That'd be pretty big if it was true. Scratch junkies didn't get cured. They cut more and more tiny holes in themselves and rode the wave until the day they died. For a minute, I wished Fortune was still alive so he could pay for this. Sure, he'd tried to stop her, tried to get her off the stuff, but once he failed, he went on sending his boys out to sell the stuff even after he knew what the scratch would do. My hands kept shaking.

She had a different memory of it. "He kept looking for ways to cure me. He didn't want to understand that it was too late. The changes are almost over now. I can feel it," she whispered, voice like scales over stones. I shuddered as she stood up but I kept looking at the ground. In my heart of hearts, I wished she had really died before I'd seen what she looked like now, and I wasn't very proud of that.

"Thanks for telling me. Goodbye, Dash." She took off so fast I wondered if the lumps on her shoulders really were wings, spreading out behind her through slits in the blue coat. I didn't look up to find out. There are some things you just don't want to see.

For the first time, I stopped to wonder if Fortune was a little better than me. He'd stuck around, watching her change into a monster, maybe even trying to fix it. I couldn't even look at her without my guts churning.

I sat there another minute, shivering against the bench, then I dragged myself to my feet and headed for the alleys. There was an old sparktag flickering its broken-bulbed message at the second one I walked past. A Kru'ush Magir blinked crookedly down to light my way, most of the bulbs in its antenna and faceted eyes broken.

Based on what the Fat Man told me, they found Fortune in one of these. I guessed that it was the one with the electriline silhouette of a body on the brick. I figured that this was far as the D. Force boys would go in their investigation. If it wasn't an alien menace or a dead Committee stooge, they didn't pay much attention. Good thing for my racket, anyway, as long as we didn't make enough noise to draw attention to ourselves.

I walked carefully around the crime scene markers and started skirting the disposals that lined the walls. There was nobody else around. I wondered what it was like at night and what the hell Fortune was doing here without muscle.

There was little shining spot under the corner of one disposal. I reached down to pick it up. It turned out to be a string of beads from an earring. More shimmers. Fortune was up to his neck in femmes from the look of it. I wondered for a minute if Leandra had iced him herself, then gave up that thought. It wasn't her. I'd seen her look at him before she'd changed. I kicked the disposal hard, then stuck the beads in my pocket with the other shimmer and poked around some more.

Nothing much turned up. A no-nic cig butt, Randall's Quality, "All of the kicks, none of the risks," like the tag says, showed up on the other side of the alley behind another disposal. Everybody from the Fat Man to Greta smoked them so I decided to leave it there since it wouldn't tell me much. Damn clean alley. Just a little dried blood and an outline to show that it wasn't always this tidy.

I headed out toward the streetcar stop, hunching my shoulders as the wind picked up and. Time to meet Greta and get a drink. Even the little bushes that lined the street looked depressed. The car showed up and I sat and made Greta slowly push Leandra out of my head. It took awhile. Hell, it felt like years.

Greta'd be coming from Studio Row. That was where they made the vids that they sold off planet, not the ones we went to every Friday. The off planet vids were in color and had more skin and blood in them. Big market for that kind of thing in the Leo II worlds. I'd been a walk-on in a few of them, something I did when business was slow. That was how I'd met her. After that, I just got lucky.

I got off the car near Sally's. The more I thought about Leandra, the more I needed a drink. Greta would check here for me when she got off the set anyway. The bug eyes and fuzzy antennae of Kru'ush Magir leered down at me from every corner. I wondered if they really looked like that and I flipped a pebble at one, cracking a bulb. It didn't help any.

The bar was a squat preconstruct wedged in between two warehouses. The plastocon bricks made it look like an Old Earth gas station, minus the windows. Nothing to tell what it was but the little red shoe on the wooden door. Those who needed to know what it meant found the place and the D. Forces left it alone most of the time. I hoped it was one of Sally's good nights. She paid plenty for them.

Vera the bouncer grinned down at me when I came in. "Howya doin', Dash?" I dodged a hearty backslap that would have staggered me and gave her my best fake grin. The one that said "my ex turned into a monster and I can't do anything about it." Her big eyes looked back, mournful now as she gave me her best shot at doggy sympathy without even knowing why.

I headed toward the bar. The place wasn't too crowded yet, and Sally, the queen of my dreams, was tending bar. The rainbow gleam of her dress flashed as the light from the open door caught it, almost blinding me. When I squinted against the glow, I could see from the makeup that we were Judy again tonight. Good. I wasn't up to Bette.

Her long face lit up with a grin until I got closer. "Hey handsome. Oops, deary, I know that look. Business not so good?" I nodded, not ready to talk about Lee. She silently poured me a gin and patted my hand while I downed the drink with the other. It had the acrid aftertaste of old zinc, like the tub out back where it was made.

Sally poured me another, then took off to wait on the boys at the end of the bar, barely wobbling on her new heels as she went. The dim lights danced over the silver glitter that coated them like they were sprinkled with pixie dust. I toasted her with my second glass and stuck a hand in my pocket for the shimmers.

There was something familiar about the earring, but right now I couldn't think what it was. I put it and the pin on the bar in front of me and just looked at them for a while. Maybe the Fat Man iced Fortune. Maybe somebody else did. Maybe Fortune was onto a cure for the scratch. Hell, maybe he was just kidding around. I wouldn't put it past him.

I downed my drink and thought about the Fat Man and Fortune, Fortune and Leandra, Leandra and the scratch. A piece fell into place. It worked if the Buggies were real. Or if Fortune thought they were.

Now I wondered if my cousin had seen who he was doing business with. Were they real Buggies or just muscle in funny costumes courtesy of the Committee? I flipped the pin over and looked at the transmitter on the other side. How the hell did he contact them? Or why pick him, if it was the other way around? My thoughts chased their tails all over the bar but didn't catch them.

Instead I got depressed staring at my reflection in the mirror over the bar. After my third gin, I decided that I didn't look too bad for a guy. Big jaw and smallish blue eyes, solid shoulders, no hips to speak of and breasts tiny enough to bind down almost flat under my Dad's old suits.

I wondered sometimes if he had known what he was doing, bringing me up as a boy. Probably. Even soused, he had been pretty clear about what he wanted. Someone had to follow in his footsteps and it wasn't going to be my sisters. Mom died before she could object so that was that. Most of the time, I could take living this particular lie but every now and then it caught up with me.

Maybe--I hated it when this occurred to me--Lee wouldn't have dumped me if I was a real guy. Maybe I should reconsider the options. I weighed the black market operation against getting my records changed and being even somewhat indebted to the Fat Man.

A couple of hours went by while I wallowed. No Greta. No answers to tonight's thousand credit questions, either. Sally switched me over to juice after my fourth gin. Said I'd just brood if she didn't. Not for the first time, I thought it was a pity she wasn't my type. I could do with someone taking care of me and Greta wasn't that girl. But then, Lee hadn't been either.

Every time Greta stood me up like this, I figured she'd had it and she was moving on for someone who could do more for her. Like Lee had. I hated that feeling. Maybe she was just working late. That's what she'd tell me when she showed up, no matter what the real story was. So I ate greasy canned meat with Vera, and played some eight ball until I couldn't take it anymore. I blew a kiss to Sally and headed out for home. Damn Greta anyway.

The old dump was only a mile or so away so I decided to walk off my mood. I stuck my hands in my pockets and pulled my hat down against the night wind and snarled every time I thought about femmes, past and present. Even the goons outside the Rialto avoided me, so I knew the tough guy routine was working for me.

It worked so well, I didn't hear them coming behind me. One good shove and I smacked up against the brick wall of the alleyway, hard. "Where's the Buggy, alien lover?" The fist that hit me in the eye made everything go black for a minute. I figured they weren't going to wait for an answer. A few more hits like the first and I was on the ground, curled up in a ball. I was trying to get my fingers inside my jacket for the raygun when the first kick caught me in the ribs.

Then the head. I went down for the count. When I woke up, I was still in the alley and it was a little before dawn. A cold rain drizzled down my nose and it hurt like hell. Probably broken. Goody. Just what I needed. I sat up slowly and the alley walls looped around in a big circle. I closed my eyes, then opened them again a few minutes later. Everything stopped moving.

So did I. I just leaned up against the wall and got wet for a while. When I tried moving again, it all still hurt but nothing was spinning. I dragged myself up on the brick and staggered home, which luckily for me, wasn't that far away. I limped up the steps and into my apartment. Or at least as far as the open door. I stuck a hand in my jacket for my gun. It was gone. Damn. I drew a deep breath and slammed the door open with my foot.

It banged against the wall and Mrs. McCreedy on the other side banged back, but that was about it. I inched inside and hit the lights. They came on and showed the world that I wasn't much of a housekeeper. Even so, I could see the place had been tossed and pretty thoroughly at that. I checked out both rooms and the closet. Nothing and no one.

Every rib howled for a glass of Sally's gin. I needed some answers but I needed to be able to move my right arm without screaming first. The bath came first. It helped but not as much as I thought it should have. Neither did breakfast.

Then I checked my pockets. My raygun wasn't the only thing missing, it turned out. The Fat Man's shimmer was gone, too. It didn't take an Einstein to figure out that it was what they were after. I had a dim memory of the goons yelling something about a "Buggy." What Buggy? And why did they think I was on speaking terms with one?

Somehow, they'd missed the earring. I pulled it out and looked at it. At that moment, I realized that I was starting to believe in the Kru'ush Magir and that was a first. Up until now, I always thought a healthy skepticism about their existence was the best policy. But right now it sure seemed like other people believed in them, at least enough to beat the tar out of me.

I opened my desk drawer and took out some old photos of Lee, more to remind myself of what she looked like before the scratch than anything else. Okay, who am I kidding? I just liked looking at her the way she was. I couldn't help noticing that she didn't favor this kind of shimmer. I stared at them for a few more minutes, then I made myself put them away before I got too down. I tried not to wonder if she still had ears.

I glanced at the photo of Greta on my desk. It took a minute. I took the bag of ice off my nose for a better look. My brain couldn't wrap itself around what I was seeing. I kept looking anyway but it didn't get any better. Maybe every femme in town had shimmers like this and I just hadn't noticed. Maybe Fortune had an ear pierced since I saw him last.

Maybe I was just kidding myself. Maybe I had been for the last three months. I tried to remember if she'd met Fortune when I'd been around but I wasn't getting a picture on that. I thought about how bad she wanted to be Femme Fatale and about how fast she'd come up through the ranks. I'd thought it was talent and looks but now I was starting to wonder. Why would a rising vid star want to go out with me, anyway?

I took the ice off my nose again. The swelling had gone down, but I was going to have a lovely shiner. The part of my brain that wasn't weeping like a baby started planning. If nothing else, I needed to replace my gun so I called my regular guy. He was all out so he recommended someone else. Johnny the shoeshine guy would be glad to oblige me. At least now I knew how he paid for the dental job. By the time I had my piece, the sun was sinking low and the two little moons, Bogie and Lorre, were starting to rise over the horizon.

I wanted to walk but there was no way my ribs were going to let me get away with that. I hopped on a streetcar and headed for the right side of the tracks and Greta's big gray house. My wingtips clicked against the concrete as I walked up the driveway and opened the gate. Looking up at the place, I could see a light on in her room.

My new raygun made a comforting lump against the few ribs that didn't hurt. I wondered how I was going to ask her about Fortune. Then I wondered about the Fat Man. There was no way he wasn't in on this. Why else would he bring me into it? I knew Fortune, I knew about the scratch and I knew...Lee. Lee who'd changed more than any scratch junky I'd ever seen and lived longer.

I decided I'd go ask. Greta If I was right, She had to be working for the Fat Man. Nothing else made sense. I wondered if he was up there in her room waiting for me, with Barney and some of his other thugs. I made myself head up the drive breathing in the stink of a setup every step of the way.

When I got to the front door, I had a little surprise. It was open. I was inside with my raygun out within two breaths. The hall was dark, and something crunched underfoot. My pulse started a quick dance tempo. I put my back to the wall and stepped lightly around the corner into the parlor. From here, I could see the bedroom light shining down the stairs.

I crept along watching the shadows. Nothing moved. Sidling up to the stairs, I started climbing, one foot after the other, not a thought in my head. Just fear, pure and simple. The bedroom was a wreck, drawers dumped, jewelry and facepaint everywhere, but that was it. The body I thought I'd see wasn't there but someone had sure packed in a hurry. My heartbeat went from a foxtrot to a waltz. All right, maybe a tango. But if she wasn't here, where was she?

I looked around some more. A gleam on the floor caught my eye. I shoved the blanket aside and found the Fat Man's shimmer, the one that the boys in the alley had taken off me. What the hell was it doing here?

All of a sudden, I wasn't sure I wanted to know. I stuck the pin in my pocket and listened to my gut. I decided to believe that Greta was safe with the Fat Man. Then I decided to leave by the fire escape and worry about it all from a few blocks away.

The beam that caught my hand on the railing wasn't set for low burn. My skin blistered as I yanked it back and rolled forward down the metal stairs, grabbed the railing at the bottom with my good hand, and jumped over it into the bushes. The shrubs were crisped behind me as I scrambled along the side of the house, aiming for the shadows and the trees out front.

I doubled around to the front of the house and the firepower got turned off. There was no good way to outrun them from here so I hunkered down to wait and listen to my hand and my ribs scream. The handlights they carried flashed on the leaves in front of me so I stayed low. My good thumb found the high setting on my raygun, and clicked it on. A brief whisper told me that they were coming. I clutched the gun and tried not to think about much of anything.

Right about then, my new friends got to the front of the house. There were four of them, led by my old pal Barney. I almost expected one of the others to be Johnny the shoeshine guy. It was that kind of night. But no, the rest were just high-class muscle.

If I got out of here, Fatso and I were going to chat. When I got out of here. Something twitched in my pocket and I pulled out the shimmer with my bad hand, gritting my teeth against the scrape of wool on burned skin. The little lights were flashing at me. I swallowed a curse and tried not to think about whether or not I'd signaled for backup and who might be receiving it.

Barney, that clever boy, seemed to think I might have headed out into the trees, never mind that they would have seen me cutting across the lawn. He and two of the goons headed over to the gate. Number four stayed about ten steps in front of me. Time to make my move. I slipped the shimmer back into my pocket. Nothing I could do about it now. I angled around a bush for a clear shot and hit him on heavy stun. Me and my soft heart.

I made it as far as the backyard when I heard a kind of crackling sound off to my right, between me and the bad guys. The blast of scorching air hit me hard, and the yells from behind me told me I wasn't the only one. A blast of raygun fire hit the hot spot and the air fired back with a reddish gold flame, not blue-white like our guns. My backup had arrived.

I started shaking but I kept moving. If I stayed, either the thugs or whatever was in that hot spot were going to get me. Just then I didn't need to know for sure whether the Kru'ush Magir looked like a sparktag or not.

A doorway shot open in the air. Another red gold flame flashed out and I could hear a scream at the other end of the lawn. I stopped moving and held my hands up. That was when she walked out, big leathery wings flowing behind her like something out of an Old Earth hell. This time, she didn't bother with a veil and her feet looked the same as the ones on her pals standing behind her. She glided over the grass until she came closer than I liked.

"Hello, Dash." I could hear her hiss around the "s."

I looked up into those big brown eyes under the thick ridges of her new face. "Hi, Lee." She didn't look much like a sparktag. It made it all worse, somehow; it would have been easier if she looked more like a Buggy. It would have made her more of an enemy. I made myself ask the obvious question. "So, are you going to tell me what all this is about?"

"You already know, don't you Dash?"

"Humor me."

"The first Committee needed something to keep itself in power after the Plague hit and things were falling apart. They thought up the Kru'ush Magir. But after a while, an imaginary enemy wasn't good enough. People were starting to ask too many questions about how no one ever saw one and our Founding Committee members couldn't have that."

"So they thought up the scratch and just rounded up the junkies when they started to change. That's why only the Defense boys ever saw one. And why they could never seem to shut down the trade." I added, lowering my arms. She didn't seem likely to shoot me just now.

"Yesss. Fortune figured it out and helped some of us hide until we got stronger and completed the change. He tried to distract the Fat Man while we broke into the D. Force's stock and stole what we needed to keep hiding. That's what got him killed."

She looked almost weepy. “It’s not over yet, Dash. Things have changed and we have you and your little Greta to thank for it. If she hadn’t iced Fortune and you hadn’t led them right to me at the market yesterday, we might have stayed in the shadows. But my friends had to come for me. No more hiding for us after that.”

I must have looked surprised. Those cold brown eyes took me in for a minute. “Yes, honey. Greta. You always suspected she’d do anything to be Femme Fatale and you were right.”

“So where is she now?” I tried not to sound too anxious, or too used.

She made a movement that looked like a shrug. “She got what wanted, at least for now. She’s probably back at Committee Headquarters making her report.” It was like a blow to the gut. Why me? I wasn’t a bad guy, not for a femme anyway.

Her raspy voice picked up again. “For the moment, I’ve got more important things to worry about. We’ll take over distribution of the scratch ourselves and decide who joins us from now on. When this war is over, we’ll run this world.” She looked as if she was waiting to see if I wanted to join the winning side but my face must have spoken for itself. She extended a claw in my general vicinity.

I reached into my pocket without a word and handed over the shimmer, being careful not to touch her scales. She took it, then grabbed my burned hand and flipped it over. Without a word, she ran a long, slightly forked tongue over it. I jerked away, feeling sick, but my skin lost its angry red glow and the blisters disappeared.

She looked me over for a minute and I knew I’d been given up as a loss. Ouch. “Goodbye, Dash.” She turned to walk back to her buddies. There were more of them then I had noticed at first. Not quite an army, but a definite start.

A sudden raygun blast broke up our little party and she knocked me flying out of its range. My head hit a rock in the grass. I'll never know if she looked back before she disappeared.

When I came to awhile later, my head hurt like hell and goon ashes were blowing across the grass. I knew had to get the hell away from here before anyone showed up to ask questions. The war would catch up with me sooner or later anyway whether I wanted it to or not. None of us would be able to stay out of it if we stayed on Falcon, not if I knew the Committee. Dragging myself to my feet, I wobbled toward the back gate that I had started for in the beginning.

Once outside on the street, I aimed for Sally's and just kept on walking. I looked at the ground so I didn't have to see the D. Force's version of the Buggies staring down at me. The Fat Man and Greta could wait until tomorrow; I knew where to find them.

If I got lucky tonight, maybe I'd meet a new femme at the bar, a nice ordinary one. Maybe we could get together before the war came home. That'd be nice. A guy like me likes to have a femme to think about when she's at the front. I shivered and walked faster.

A Day at the Inn, A Night at the Palace

Morning hit me like a kick from my horse. I thought about summoning a shriek of despair as I opened my eyes, but it was clear that it would hurt too much. Besides, somewhere nearby someone else was groaning enough for both of us.

First I wondered why I let Raven get me into this, whatever this was, even without knowing how my cousin was involved. Then I squinted against the light pouring in through what appeared to be wooden shutters and took a slow, cautious look around. The room looked familiar, in a many tankards later, I-wish-I-was-still asleep sort of way. There were tables, benches and the smell of stale beer and overworked swordswoman. Ah, that I recognized.

But there was something else too. A flowery scent of clean, well-dressed highborn lady hung in the air in a perfume cloud. That was…unusual, given the kind of women I usually woke up with. All the more so as my foggy mind had recognized the room I was lying in. Highborn ladies did not come to an inn like The Sodden Rat, and that in itself was most wise of them.

I widened my squint and looked around. Raven was nowhere to be seen. But on my swordarm side, buried amidst a mound of pink silk, I could see another familiar face. What in the Seven Hells was Her Highness Princess Miaqi-Tan Sera doing here?

We had had a brief audience with Her Highness two nights ago. She summoned us to a secret meeting to discuss the possibility of her assuming her father's throne upon his death. There was one minor inconvenience, that being that her older brother stood between her and the throne. This was the problem that we were supposed to correct on her behalf.

We had turned the job down, with Raven employing his most flowery and careful phrasing. It wasn't so much that we loved the idea of spendthrift, drunken and cruel Prince Herali on the throne as it was that we didn't think Miaqi could succeed her father. "She lacks the requisite force of mind to slaughter her family and hold the throne once the deed was done," Raven had said thoughtfully when we were out of earshot. "Though I admire her enthusiasm."

I had agreed, with some regret. I was curious to see what would happen. But I had no great enthusiasm for turning assassin. Raven and I were mercenaries, soldiers, occasionally thieves out of necessity, but that was the limit of our skills. In any case, meddling in the affairs of the Sunborn generally caused one to wind up dead sooner rather than later. I had no desire to see the Lady's caves before my time either.

And yet, here the Princess was again. Only this time, we were lying on the floor of the main room of the Rat and I had no memory of how either of us had gotten here. Or where Raven was. I dragged myself onto my hands and knees and crawled over to her. "Your Highness," I began carefully. "Your Highness, are you all right?"

One amber eye opened and gazed at me with a startling amount of recognition. It was oddly flattering. Normally, women noticed Raven and not me. At least at first. "Highness?" she croaked. "Nice to hear you giving me the respect I deserve, little cousin."

"Cousin?" I sat up and stared down at her. Raven and I came from minor nobility in the outlying provinces, but I was quite certain that we were not related to any of the court Sunborn. Perhaps it was some kind of affectionate term? Or a joke? I wished Raven was here. He was much better with delirious women than I was.

I tried again. "Princess Miaqi? Are you able to move?"

That seemed to revive her. Both amber eyes shot open and she sat up straight, an expression of pure horror twisting her pretty face. Her beringed fingers went to her round breasts, then swept downward over the lush curve of her hips beneath the silk of her dress. Something about that exploration seemed unexpected. "Seven Hells! What's happened to me?" She stared at me, wild-eyed.

"I'm not sure, Highness. I am surprised as you are to find myself here at your side." I pulled myself slowly to my feet. "I don't suppose you know where my cousin Raven is?"

"Where I am? I'm in front of you!"

It was worse than I thought. Princess Miaqi's quest for the throne had led to madness. Very sudden madness. Now what was I supposed to do? I was a fighter, not a nursemaid. "Perhaps I could fetch you some ale, Princess? Help you to sit up?"

"It's me, Maeve. Can't you tell that it's me?" Princess Miaqi's delicate tapered fingers buried themselves in her long black hair. I found that I wanted to do the same, consequences be damned.

No, Maeve, no. Do not entertain fantasies about the beautiful but unfortunate and clearly deranged Sunborn. Those lead to dungeons and beheadings. "Why don't you let me help you up to a bench?" I stood, still swaying a bit myself and tried to sound soothing.

Princess Miaqi lurched upward at the same time, one thin arm flailing out to catch herself on a nearby table. "Listen, Maeve, cousin, do you remember when we left Tacred? Do you remember what I said when you told me you could never marry me? Do you remember that I said we should come here and pledge our swords to the King?"

Yes, he'd said that. And he'd said that he felt the same way about marrying me. We'd stolen my brother's swords and run away that night.

Now, it was my turn to look astonished. I hadn't left Raven alone with the Princess so he couldn't have told her about us. True, the scandal of our supposed elopement, then subsequent failure to marry, had been quite notorious for a time. In Tacred, which was the size of a farmer's field. That alone should have kept the news well away from Miaqi's ears. "Go on," I said at last, though without enthusiasm.

"We ran away with me dressed in your girl's clothes because I was more believable as a maiden than you were. No one knows that except for you and me, right?" She was staring at me with a pleading expression in those golden eyes now. And she was right, I had never told anyone else that story and guessed that Raven had not either, which left one other possibility…

"Raven?" I could hear the uncertainty in my voice. "Why you look like Princess Miaqi?" Maybe it was just a glamour. My cousin had recently discovered his talent for magic and was trying to hone it. He must have been practicing and something went wrong. That was it. I leaned against a table and waited for a reasonable explanation.

"I don't *look* like Princess Miaqi! I *am* Princess Miaqi!" Miaqi wailed and buried her face in her hands.

This was going to end well.

And if it was true, we were in horrible, horrible trouble. I groaned and tried again to think through the haze that still filled my brain, so, of course, I thought about our past. We'd set out from Tacred to do great deeds but somehow it hadn't worked out that way. A few days ago, I'd have said that we both needed a change, to do something besides sell our sword skills. Raven's interest in magic was proof enough of that. But this was more of a change than I had in mind. A lot more.

"Should I call you 'Raven' then?" One amber eye glared at me between parted fingers. "Right. Raven, it is. Do you remember what happened?" I gestured toward the princess' curvy form. The round soft curve of her breasts, the gentle sweep of her rounded hips, the…yes, we were in horrible, horrible trouble.

The Rat's potboy wandered in from the kitchen, rubbed his eyes and blinked. Then stood there open-mouthed. You would think he had never seen a Sunborn princess up close and personal before.

Even in my less than alert state, it didn't take much time to realize that if the Princess was here, she was missing from the Palace. And from there. I could work out who was most likely to be blamed for how she got here. We needed somewhere to talk in private. Now. "My cousin's just created an illusion, lad. Nothing to stare at, though he's well worth a second look." I tossed him a copper. "Hold your tongue and there's another in it for you. Now, who's upstairs?"

He stumbled through a list of cutthroats and scum who I wouldn't consider waking up with Raven-as-Princess in tow until he got to a familiar name. Roderick the Many-Handed was a Palace Guard now. But before he got respectable, he had been a mercenary and we had all fought together in the ill-fated invasion of the neighboring kingdom of Serest.

Hopefully, he'd remember enough of the good old days to hold his tongue for a few hours while I figured out what to do next. Or maybe he'd have some useful advice. In any case, I didn't have a better idea.

I grabbed Miaqi's arm and towed her toward the stairs. "Upstairs, Prin—er, Raven. Let's go visit an old friend."

"What are you doing? You can't mean…" Miaqi ran out of breath as I herded her up the stairs. Apparently, the Princess wasn't in full fighting trim, which would make my life easier for the moment. I shoved her down the hallway as gently as I could, listening for the tell tale signs of Roderick's snore at each dilapidated doorway.

"What are you doing, Maeve? Don't you remember what happened the last time Roderick and I met?" I did remember, but I thought we had bigger problems now. Miaqi, all right, *Raven*, looked as if she wanted to bolt back down the stairs. Fortunately, I was still holding her arm. It wasn't like Roderick would skewer Raven on sight regardless of which body he was in. I hoped.

I knocked on the door that sounded like the best possibility. "Rod? You in there?" No answer. I knocked again, this time hearing the ominous silence that indicates that an opponent is now waiting with a drawn sword on the other side of a closed door to see what you'll do next. I shoved the Princess out of the way and kicked the door hard.

It slammed open, then just as quickly slammed shut. A distinctly unRoderick feminine squeal wafted forth. He'd be extra pleased to see the Princess and me since he had company. I tried not to dwell on that thought as I yanked my sword free of its scabbard and waited for what I knew would follow. The door shot open again and there was clash of blades as Roderick's sword met mine.

I parried his thrusts twice before he recognized me. "Maeve? What are you doing here with…Your Highness?" His sword dropped to a more discrete position. Roderick the Many-Handed was quite impressively naked. "Did you kidnap--"

"Who're they?" His companion joined him in the doorway, wearing a torn shift that might have once been white. She had long red hair and big brown eyes and was looking at me with great interest.

I looked back with equal interest, but settled for a small bow of acknowledgment. "Corporal Maeve the Red, swordswoman, last of the Prince of Surest's Company, at your service." From behind me, I could hear Raven snicker. Like it wasn't the same thing he tried on every barmaid we met.

"Ginn. Of the Rat." Her gaze swept me over again, this time with a bit more warmth. I wondered if she was seeing my body, broader and stronger than that of most men. Or just the ugly scar that ran the length of my cheek, souvenir of a duel fought years ago. I shrugged the thought off and looked at Rod.

He growled something that had clearly started out as an oath before it got bitten off. "Maeve, why is Her Highness Princess Miaqi-Tan Sera standing in the hallway behind you?"

It was a reasonable question. If only I had a reasonable answer. "Let an old swordsister in, Roderick. I need to get her out of sight for the moment. I'll explain once we're inside."

Rod actually blushed. But he stepped back. I took the opportunity to grab the Princess' arm and push her forward into the room, only a moment later realizing that I was still having trouble thinking of her as Raven. Ginn handed Rod his trousers and shut the door. I admired her presence of mind, among other things. It was a very thin shift.

Raven poked me sharply in the back. "Now what?"

It was an excellent question. Rod turned away and was pulling his trousers on but his companion was still watching us. Raven sighed and walked over to the bed, sitting on its edge with an audible thump. "Let's get this over with. I'm not who I appear to be."

Roderick turned around and ran a hand through his thinning black hair. None of us were getting any younger. My own years were weighing on me like plate armor today. Still, I held up a hand to stop any further discussion and tilted my head toward the girl. The fewer who knew what had happened to Miaqi, the better. Rod clearly understood my meaning but shrugged.

Ginn looked from him to me and gave me an impish grin. "Oh no, I'm not leaving unless you throw me out. And then I'll make so much noise the Guards will show up to see what's going on. I want to hear this." She looked at Raven expectantly.

Raven buried her face in her hands and groaned. "What's one more? So a little while ago, we woke up downstairs on the floor--"

Ginn made a disgusted sound and I noticed that Rod was now standing at attention, sword at his side. The fact that he still didn't have his shirt on made it less impressive than it might have been. The rigidity lasted right up until Raven told the rest of the story, "Last night, I was Raven Foesbane and this morning, I'm Princess Miaqi Tan-Sera."

If I hadn't been waiting for Rod to make his move, things might have ended badly. Well, they were still likely to but at least I bought us more time. My blade caught his mid swing and I ducked under the whoosh of the blade in his other hand. He wasn't called "Many-Handed" for nothing. "Rod!" I shouted to get his attention.

All of which was focused on Raven/Miaqi. I was just an obstacle, at least until I kicked him sharply in the leg. "Ow!" Roderick the Many-Handed glared at me.

"Stop it," I said firmly. "We need to figure out why this happened and how to turn him back. Then you can fight him."

"That's easy," Ginn spoke up. We all looked at her with varying degrees of disbelief. "It is. I mean the why this happened part. Everyone knows the Sunborn are fighting each other for the throne. What better disguise for the Princess than a new body?" She shrugged. "Her brother won't know what hit him."

Raven/Miaqi stared at me. "Then when I get my body back, I'll be--"

"The assassin who killed the heir to the throne?" I offered.

"And on the block," Rod helpfully finished my thought with a slash across his throat. He looked a lot more cheerful now. It was nice to see that Raven's charm was holding up, regardless of what form he took.

The look the Princess gave me was pure Raven. "We've got to stop her."

"Well, she'll want her old body back sooner or later." Ginn shrugged. We all looked at her again, this time with a lot less disbelief. "She can't take the throne as someone else, after all. She's got to be the Princess again."

"Which means we were put here for safe keeping. But if I wanted to make sure my body was available to switch back to when I wanted it, I'd also make sure that someone was keeping an eye on it." I stared suspiciously at Roderick.

He picked up his uniform shirt and shrugged. "You came to me, remember?"

"Alright." There was nothing I could do about it right now anyway. "The question is how do we stop her?" I looked, not at Raven like I usually did, but at Ginn. She gave me another appraising glance that nearly made me blush.

"We have to get into the palace," Raven said in flutelike tones. He stood up and began to pace back and forth, long pink gown tripping him up in the tiny room. Rod and I backed up and the girl went to sit on the bed. We all watched the Princess who was not a Princess walk with Raven's strides. It was getting easier to believe that Raven was in there, somewhere.

"What makes you think that's where she'll be?" I asked, just because no one else had. I looked around to see if anyone else was wondering.

Rod was clearly intrigued and annoyed at himself for it. Soon he would be annoyed at Raven again and I wasn't looking forward to that.

It did make me wonder if we could keep Raven in Miaqi's body for awhile longer, long enough so that every other fighter, thief and mercenary in the city who he'd ever cheated out of their winnings or whose mistress he'd bedded forgot who he was. But we'd both die of old age before that happened. I sighed and resigned myself to storming the Sunborn's palace instead.

"I know that she'll be there because her brother is there. The King is dying. The whole kingdom knows that. What better time and place to remove her rival?" Raven dragged his pink train out of the way and swore. "I need new clothes!"

"Done," Ginn shimmied out of her shift and handed it over. "I'll trade."

"They say," Rod added, clearly distracted, "that the mage Keranin is her lover..." He trailed off.

I looked at Ginn and it was my turn to look appraising. Rod had excellent taste. And it was clear that Raven was too stunned to take much notice, which told me all I needed to know. If he failed to notice a pretty woman, then I'd need to do more of the planning than usual. In general, strategy was his strong point, fighting was mine. But this was not that day. More changes, all of them quite unwelcome so far.

I scowled out the window, then back at Ginn. And like magic, and much as I was enjoying the view, I had an idea. If we could pass as palace servants, we might be able to figure out where Miaqi was and what she and this mage Keranin had done to steal Raven's body. Servants know everything. "I think we can get into the palace unnoticed if we can disguise you, Raven. Especially if we have some help." I stared meaningfully at Rod, who scowled back.

"Why should I risk my commission to help Raven? I like him better the way he is now." Rod leered suggestively and Raven flushed crimson, eyes flashing.

Ginn went over to help Raven out of the dress, if by "help," we meant remove with a speed and enthusiasm that stopped just short of tearing the delicate silk. A few moments later, Raven was wearing the dirty shift and Ginn looked like a cross between a scullery maid and a princess. I liked the transition enough to wink at her. She handed Raven a grubby dress to put over the shift and smiled at me.

"Is that good enough to pass for one of the lower palace servants?" I asked Rod, gesturing at the dress. We'd have to steal better clothes somewhere along the way but this might be enough to get us inside.

"Yes," Ginn said decisively. She held out her hand for the Princess' jewelry.

"No," said Rod, with equal certainty.

"Well? Which one is it?" I wanted a mug of ale. More importantly, I wanted the gold to buy myself enough ale to forget that any of this had ever happened. I wasn't likely to get either of those things any time soon and the knowledge was making me impatient and angry. The next step after that involved demonstrating how I'd earned the "Red" part of my name. I took a deep breath and tried not to explode.

"It's enough to get you into the kitchens. That's where my sister works as a pit and ash girl. If you want to get close to the Sunborn upstairs, you need a uniform so you'll have to steal those." Ginn was sweeping back and forth in the pink silk, twisting around to admire her posterior.

I admired it too and wondered how good her information was. The pit and ash cleaners were the lowest of the kitchen servants, not worth wasting a uniform on. And there wouldn't be a lot of them, unlike say, maids, so it would be harder to pass without notice either in the kitchens or outside them.

That sent me off into wondering what difference it made if we were noticed or not when we didn't know where we were going to do in the palace, once we got there. The tromp of boots on cobblestones outside the window interrupted my reverie. I glanced outside and down at a squad of Guards who were marching up to the Rat's door. There was only reason that I could think of for them to be there.

Raven's eyes rolled like a frightened horse's and Ginn stripped off the silk gown. She stuffed it up the chimney of the crumbling fireplace with a skill that suggested long practice with hiding things from the Guards. Then she hid a necklace and some rings in the straw, slipped under the blanket and beckoned to Rod. "Rub soot on her face and just walk out like you woke up with your lightskirt. Go to the palace kitchen and look for El. That's my sister; tell her I said to help you if she can," she said as if she'd done this before too. Which, perhaps, she had.

Then she winked at me. I thought about winking back, but it seemed like too much of a promise. I might not be back this way.

Though I surprised myself by how much I wanted to be sure I would be doing just that.

Instead I grabbed some grime from the fireplace and rubbed it on Raven's face. He pulled me out of the room as Ginn kissed Rod with evident enthusiasm. A sharp pang went through me at the sight, but this was not the time to linger.

Raven was messing up his hair and biting his lip when I looked his way. He reached out and seized my arm just as the first of the Guards marched up the stairs. A high-pitched giggle filled the air. "Oh, you're so strong! Buy a girl an ale and some bread now. It's the least you can do after wearing me out like that." It took me a moment to realize that the voice was coming from Raven. He fluttered Miaqi's lashes at me and simpered as he molded his body to my side as much as my armor permitted.

It was…distracting. And disturbing. Miaqi was lovely, certainly, but I hadn't really wanted to bed her when she was in possession of her own body. The fact that I was even somewhat tempted now with my cousin in residence didn't bear too much scrutiny.

But the Guard captain was in front of us, oversized face set in a near permanent scowl. "State your names and your purpose here."

Raven simpered and fluttered even more. Then thrust his bosom out further than even I thought possible and said, "I'm Venna and I'm a serving wench at the Boar. This is the mighty warrior Maeve the Red. Surely you've heard of her! As for our purpose, well, Captain, I'm sure you can guess." More giggles. I looked stern and solemn, or at least I thought that's what I was doing, which meant I probably looked like a slightly confused horse.

The Captain peered at me. "Maeve the Red, eh? I thought you'd be taller."

My hand went to the hilt of my sword and he stepped back. "Are we done, Captain? I have an appointment to keep." I went for a slightly menacing tone in case the sword hilt wasn't enough of a hint. He nodded, face a bit paler, and we walked down the hallway and marched down the stairs as the Guards began banging on doors. I heard mutters of "Where in the Hells is she?" from behind us and hid a grin. At least we were off to a good start.

Then I remembered that I was wearing my leather armor and a sword. Precisely the sort of thing that kitchen pit and ash cleaners didn't wear, as far as I knew. "I need to hide my sword and armor," I muttered to Raven as we walked through yet more Guards. He giggled vacantly, which I took for agreement, then began steering me slightly away from the palace. I wondered where we were going now.

A few steps and a couple of alleys later and I no longer had that question. Now it was my turn to stare at Raven as if he had lost all his senses. "No. I'll never see it any of it again if I leave it with her and you know how I feel about this sword."

Raven's expression on Miaqi's face was jarring, to say the least. "Maeve, I want my body back. I want it now. We can't get into the palace if you're dressed like that. This is just until we come back."

"What makes you think we're coming back?" I growled. Magic always made me nervous. You never knew when your opponent might turn into a snake or an ogre or fly away. Or turn you into something. I had a squad leader once who got turned into a puddle of horse piss by a battle mage. It was very upsetting. Not to mention messy. But I was digressing because I definitely didn't want to leave my armor and sword with…

"I knew you'd be back." The woman on the doorstep might have been Ginn's mother, from her looks, if I hadn't known better. I always did like redheads. "You just can't stay away, can you?" Then she noticed Raven. "And you brought a new friend. Interesting."

"Mirna. I hadn't thought to find myself with you again so soon. This is a happy accident...of sorts. Allow me to present my cousin, Kiru, who's come to visit from Tacred. Like a little sister she is to me." I hugged Raven in an aggressively friendly manner that aped that of my own brothers and hoped it would be enough to draw attention from her.

It seemed to be. Mirna dismissed Raven to focus on me. I squirmed slightly. "And you want something. What is it now, Maeve? My best years weren't enough for you?"

"It was two moons between campaigns three seasons ago, Mirna. You kicked me out because your husband was coming back, the way I remember it. But I have missed you," I tried to ape one of Raven's expressions. He poked me hard in the back by way of a hint to hurry up. "May we come in?"

It took longer than either Raven or I wanted, but then, Mirna was right. I had missed a few things about her. And those things took time. Even so, before nightfall we were on our way to the palace kitchens. Mirna saw us out with a smile and some of her husband's clothes, which fit me well enough to let me pass for a pit cleaner if no one looked too closely.

They didn't. I had become too used to being Maeve the Red, known for being able to kill a man before he had drawn three breaths. I was feared, sometimes even desired, but always noticed. Now I wasn't and I didn't like it much.

Raven, on the other hand, sashayed down the street flirting with every passing man as if the Sunborn's Guards weren't looking for him. He was, I reflected as I glared at him, behaving exactly like the sort of girl he flirted with and bedded in every tavern and market stall in every town we ever traveled through.

Dignity was clearly too much to expect. I hardly felt like I knew him any more.

On the other hand, no one would recognize him as Princess Miaqi, at least not until we got close enough to the palace for someone to recognize her face. I wondered if the mage and the Princess really were lovers. If Miaqi's face was recognized, maybe we could get captured and brought to the mage that much faster. Or killed sooner. Upon reflection, I decided not to mention this notion to Raven.

The palace was at the very center of the city, perched on the highest hill and surrounded by the houses of rich merchants and nobles. Hired household swords watched us carefully from doorsteps and guard posts. Servants in livery sneered at us as we walked steadily upward toward the rear gate of the palace. Even I was thoroughly ashamed of us by the time we got there.

"You look like a very believable pit and ash man, cousin." Raven muttered from the corner of his very pink lips. We had joined the end of a lengthy procession that was wending its way under the stone walls and through the portcullis.

"That's what will keep my head on my shoulders for the moment, cousin. See if you can do the same."

Certainly the guards at the gates seemed to believe we were who we said we were. Their hands roved so freely over Raven that I thought we would end by fighting our way in, but he clenched his jaw and forced out a smile and a few giggles. I wondered if he'd learn something from this; his hands were certainly free enough with women when he was in his own body. I looked forward to living long enough to ask.

Eventually, we were allowed to pass and make our way through the endless courtyards and corridors of the palace to its kitchens. Raven poked me hard every time he thought I didn't look enough like a servant. I poked him back every time I could get away with it and we were both sore by the time we reached the kitchen door. There a red-faced cook greeted us with a bellow, "You! Why are you late?"

Raven started to reply, only to get shoved toward the fireplace by the cook's meaty paw. My turn came next. "Turn the spit, you fool! Can't you see the meat is starting to burn?"

Now that he mentioned it, I could see it. I took my place at one side of the vast pit and began turning as Raven started shoveling ash. Apparently, our disguises had worked, at least for the cook. The woman shoveling ashes next to Raven looked puzzled though. "Ginn sent us," Raven hissed, presumably taking a guess based on the girl's red hair.

"Did she now?" We both got a crooked grin. "She must not like you much. You'll be at this all night."

"We can't stay!" Now I was hissing. "We have to find the King's mage."

"Well, he won't be passing through here," she laughed, as if the notion was entertaining.

"That's why we need to get to him," Raven repeated patiently. "Where are his rooms?"

"What do you want with him anyway? Turn you into a puddle of horse-piss if you anger him, or so it's said." There was more shoveling while I shuddered and kept turning the meat. Then there was a shower of curses from the cook, the junior cooks and some others I couldn't identify. We were quiet for a while.

Finally Raven spoke up again. "Have you ever heard anything about him being able to shift into other bodies? Do the servants speak of such things?"

She raised an eyebrow. "The 'servants'? Unlike, say, your gracious lord and lady selves?" She took in our clothes at a glance. "But you aren't what you seem to be, then, are you. Are you here to assassinate him?"

I intervened, seeing as my cousin appeared about to agree, "No. He stole...something of ours. We need to steal it back." It was as good a description of our current circumstances as I could muster on the spot. Raven gave me a begrudging nod that tilted Miaqi's tresses into the firelight and made our new friend jump and narrow her eyes.

"Right. I wonder what it was that he took. And if I should curtsey and scrape or perhaps scream for the Guards." El kept looking at Raven who tried his most charming and innocent smile on her. It didn't work as well on Miaqi's features. El frowned suspiciously.

"Please help us," I said finally. "All we want is to take back what was ours, then leave the palace. Nothing more than that. We won't get you into trouble," As I said it, I finally began to wonder just how we were going to get Raven's true form back. It wasn't like the mage was simply going to wave a hand and switch everyone back the way they had been, after all. Not without persuasion in some form. I wondered if Raven had thought that part through. I knew I hadn't.

"That seems like a lot." But she shrugged and stopped frowning. "But it's your doom. Through that doorway, up the first four flights of stairs, three corridors west, two corridors north, then up more stairs, if you can get past the corridor guards and the footmen and maids. Then I think you can get to the stairs to the wizard's tower." She bent back over the ashes with a tired grace.

Raven jerked his head at the cooks and gave me a meaningful look. I wasn't sure exactly what it was supposed to tell me, but I thought I could guess. Shoving El aside from the fire and tossing a flaming log across the floor to create a distraction was the work of moments and singed fingers.

A chorus of yells and much scrambling from cooks and kitchen servants and we were through the door at the far end of the kitchen. The corridor was full of yet more servants and we hung our heads and tried to look as if we were on an errand of some sort.

From the stories that the bards tell, you'd think it was easy to get your hands on a disguise in a palace full of people. What they seem to forget is that palaces are indeed full of people. Very few convenient dark corridors, everyone with an errand to run or a place to guard. It makes it quite difficult to knock out a couple of servants and steal their uniforms.

We did eventually make our way to the upper floors in ill-fitting livery, hoping that the mage's rooms were obvious and easy to find. Or at least, that was what I was hoping. Raven was wearing a maid's uniform and the oddest expression on his face. He remembered to duck his head and look away whenever we passed a guard or servants, but otherwise, he was clearly somewhere else.

The other thing that those ballads of daring rescues and so forth fail to note is just how very long it takes to get from the lower levels of a palace to the upper ones. It felt like a forced march through the northern mountains after a while: down endless corridors, up steep staircases that went from wood to stone as we climbed higher. Eventually, I stopped one of the maids to ask where we were, over Raven's whispered objections.

The nervous looking maid told me enough that I was able to lead us up another corridor to the bottom of yet another winding flight of stairs. This one led, inevitably, upward to the one of the towers. "Towers," Raven murmured. "Why does it always have to be towers?"

He had a point. Wizards and mages usually took the high ground. Presumably because it made it easier to see your enemies coming, but I guessed there was more to it than that. But it wasn't as if I knew any wizards personally and could ask them. Except Raven, and he wasn't a real wizard.

Or was he? That thought made me take a long look at my cousin. It was partially because he was much more fun to look at this way than he normally was, but also because for the first time I wondered what kind of wizard he would make. If he were a real wizard. Up until now, I hadn't seen him do much with his supposed powers except to charm a few dice. And I had my doubts about that.

He must have been thinking along the same lines since he stopped and held his hand over the stairs and closed his eyes like he was expecting something to happen. I noticed a ring on his finger that I hadn't seen there before. I wondered where it had come from. He moved Miaqi's lips silently while I tried to look as if this what we were supposed to be doing. Fortunately, the armies of servants and guards who filled the lower corridors seemed to be giving this one a wide berth.

A pale green glow lit Raven's fingertips for an instant. Then it faded and he slumped against the stone wall. Now the questions poured from my lips in a flood of nervous chatter, "When did you learn to do that? What's it supposed to do? I thought we were going to head up there and hold the wizard at swords point until he changes you back. You know, what we usually do."

He opened Miaqi's eyes in a catlike glare. "We don't have any swords right now, Maeve," he said in a dangerously reasonable voice. "What we do have is some pretty bad disguises, our wits and my magic. What's upstairs," he pointed upward, "is a mage who can change me into this." He gestured at Miaqi's curves.

"We need something more. I'm trying to see if I can find out something about him before we go up there."

"Actually, what's waiting for you upstairs is the least of your worries right now." Raven's voice came from behind us, echoing against the walls. I spun around, reaching for a sword that wasn't there. Then I struck out as hard as I could with my fist. Princess Miaqi Tan-sera stepped aside, laughing and I missed.

Of course, she had a sword and it was held in Raven's hand as if it had always been there. She pointed it at us and gestured upwards, the look in her eyes unmistakable. Apparently, she'd found that ruthless edge that she had lacked before. How fortunate for us. We started up the steps ahead of her, her blade a fingers-breadth from Raven's throat.

My head whirled with strategies, each formulated, then dismissed almost as quickly as they arrived. If I fought Miaqi on the stairs, I might win, even without a sword. But then how would we get Raven back into his own body? I kept climbing and tried not to think too hard about what would happen if we couldn't get out of this.

When we got to the top of the stairs, Miaqi poked me in the back with the sword, which I now recognized as Raven's second best. From the look on his face, he had already noticed. "Open the door." Her tone, combined with Raven's customarily arrogant-sounding voice, was enough to make my blood heat.

But that made no difference. We still didn't have a plan. So I improvised.

I opened the door and stepped inside fast, hoping to find a weapon or at least a good vantage point for an attack. It might have worked if she hadn't thrown Raven in after me, knocking me to my knees when he landed on top of me.

"That's quite an entrance." The voice came from somewhere above me, but I was having trouble hearing over Raven's cursing, not to mention seeing through the mane of Miaqi's hair that now covered my eyes.

Raven tumbled off my back and I looked up into the thin face and mildly surprised expression of a much younger man than I was expecting. In fact, he looked too young to have a beard. Certainly too young to be a King's mage, though I could see dried herbs and the requisite mysterious bowls on the tables around the room behind him.

Miaqi stepped forward, after shutting and bolting the door behind her. "Apparently this fool and his companion decided to save us the trouble of finding them when it is time to change me back." She sneered at Raven, who scrambled to his feet, a snarl twisting Miaqi's features. I caught his arm before he lunged at her.

"Why not change them back now?" I asked in my most reasonable voice. "Seeing as we're all here."

Miaqi laughed. It was Raven's laugh, but she managed to make her own. I didn't like it much. Surprisingly enough, neither did her wizard. I could see Keranin frown from the edge of my eye as I watched the Princess. Perhaps that could be useful.

"And why would I want to do that? My brother still lives. You're a woman, you know how it is to be overlooked, your talents disregarded." She gave me a burning stare, then glanced at the wizard as if for confirmation. "I will change back when I'm done with him, not a moment sooner."

Raven gave her a look of pure disbelief, then looked at me as if to see whether I'd deny it. Considering that our families had nearly forced us to wed because they thought it would make me give up the sword, expecting me to deny Miaqi's words was rather foolish of him.

In general, no, I wasn't overlooked. But then I was taller than many men and was one of the most feared swordswomen in the Sunborn Realms. That didn't stop some of our brethren from assuming that Raven was more deadly with a blade than I and testing me until I drew blood. I could only imagine what it would be like to be passed over for the throne by a brutal and incompetent sot simply because he was my older brother and therefore innately worthy of the throne.

Though I wasn't entirely sure yet that she would be an improvement, I ignored Raven and nodded cautiously at the Princess. There was no harm in pretending that I could be won over. Perhaps I could. She did, after all, have both sword and mage on her side.

Speaking of which, I wondered how the mage felt about Miaqi's quest for the throne. Right now, he was looking at her with an odd expression on his face. I studied his face and the emotions flickering across it. He was fine-boned, with dark brown skin that suggested an origin in the western mountains of the far kingdoms. Beneath the gold and blue robe that he wore, he was slender, not much taller than Miaqi herself. There was also something familiar in the way that he moved.

Apparently it dawned on Raven at the same time. "You're not what you appear to be, either," my cousin said, stepping closer to the mage with narrowed eyes. The mage stepped back, her fingers beginning to glow.

"Enough!" Miaqi barked.

I stepped between them, then cursed the impulse that made me do it. Under other circumstances, it might have been fun to watch my cousin get his comeuppance at the hands of a beautiful princess and her female mage. But not if he got turned into a puddle of horse piss in the process. So there I was, in the middle of it all, but still without an idea of what to do next.

I tried diplomacy. "All right. We've all got our secrets. What if we help you defeat your brother? Then you switch bodies with Raven and ascend the throne as yourself. My cousin and I will forget all this ever happened and join the campaign on the Southern border." It was a safe thing to say; there was always a campaign on the Southern border.

"When M—Her Highness ascends the throne, there will be no more war on the Southern border," the mage's voice was clear and high, and not surprisingly, like a girl's. The mage and the princess exchanged a look and the latter stood up a bit straighter.

Well, now we knew how the mage felt about Miaqi's quest for the throne. Raven and I exchanged a glance of our own. A Sunborn ruler with a peaceful agenda was something new and potentially troublesome. But Raven didn't look worried. In fact, he gave me a tiny wink. Evidently, he thought he had a plan. I looked from him to the mage. Her face appeared to be bright with hope and love, all of it directed at the Princess.

Idealists. I nearly shook my head. Still, I couldn't help myself from trying to imagine what the kingdom would look like if there were no campaign on the Southern border. Or elsewhere. And what I would do if I didn't live by my sword? It was a troubling, but not unappealing thought.

Unbidden, the Rat and a certain red-haired serving girl came to mind. Perhaps I did know what I might do, were there no more campaigns. Then again, perhaps idealism was contagious. I shook my head. Time enough to worry about that when we got Raven back to being Raven.

My cousin tapped my foot impatiently with his. He was telling the Princess and her mage that he had a plan to get Miaqi on the throne. It involved kidnapping and magic and changing the Prince into someone else. I stopped listening halfway through when it became clear that it was too elaborate to pull off without an army, which we didn't have.

I could see that the Princess thinking something similar. Every time the plan took another twist, she frowned but I couldn't see any confusion or puzzlement on what would normally have been Raven's face. I liked her better for her pragmatism but I wondered whether she could come up with something better.

I also wondered how long it would take for the Prince to realize that his sister was up to something and simply kill us all out of hand. It would be the most efficient thing to do. It would be what I would do in his shoes. I decided it was time to ask if anyone else had the same thought. "What will the Prince be doing while we're running around the palace switching bodies and so forth? He's not a complete idiot. His advisors will suspect you're up to something, even if he doesn't," this last said to the Princess and the mage.

"And my father is dying. Whatever we do, we do now before it's too late." Miaqi set Raven's lips in a thin line. Determination sat well on his features. I hadn't seen it for quite a while. There had been a time, right after we arrived in the Sunborn's city that both of us had ideals, had dreams of serving a great and noble prince and doing legendary deeds. It turned out to be harder than we thought. Too many campaigns had come and gone since then for those dreams to survive intact, leaving us tired, dissipated and cynical.

Still, I thought I was finding a spark of my former self tonight. "How did you change them?" I asked the mage, gesturing at Raven and the Princess. "Is it something you could do from a distance?" The glimmers of something approaching a plan were dancing around in my head.

She looked at Miaqi as if for permission or something like it. The Princess said nothing. I couldn't blame them. Once we knew how they did it, we could probably figure out a way to do it ourselves. Raven swore angrily and stepped up to the table, fingers glowing pale green once more. Evidently that had been his plan.

I grabbed his shoulder and shook him a little, and the glow faded.

"Wait." I looked at the mage again. She gave me an intent stare back, her lips thin with anger, or perhaps her version of determination. Raven's arm quivered beneath my hand, drawing my attention back to him. "We'll need something different." I could feel his fury building, even in the wrong body.

"I was unaware that you had a choice in the matter," Princess Miaqi Tan-sera nearly growled the words. "We need to end this tonight. To do that, we need to find my brother."

"And how will you make sure we're the ones who are blamed for the deed?" Raven said softly, an edge to his tone.

I read guilt in the mage's face and some of my newfound enthusiasm ebbed away. She glanced up and murmured, "You would have done the same."

Since it wouldn't have occurred to me, I wouldn't have done it, but this didn't seem the time to mention that. I was beginning to hear noises outside the tower. Noises that sounded suspiciously like armed men moving in the courtyard, being as quiet as one can in armor. "Is there another way out of here besides the stairs? I think we'll have company soon."

Again, the mage and the princess exchanged glances, then the mage beckoned us forward. "Over here." She pulled back a tapestry and gestured to what seemed to be blank stone. Raven swore under his breath as it was made clear that we needed to turn away so that we wouldn't know how to open the tower's secret entrance. Then both mage and princess busied themselves finding a latch of some sort.

From the corner of my eye, I saw Raven's hand dart out to grab something on one of the tables then vanish into his clothes.

I did a small amount of pilfering of my own, palming a bag with a slight metal jingle to it. Of course, we both watched the mage and the princess so we could find the latch when we needed it.

Then a door behind one of the tapestries slid open. We followed the mage into the secret stairwell while Miaqi followed on our heels, pulling everything shut behind her. "So," I asked quietly as we made our way down the stairs, "the first plan was to attack and assassinate your brother in Raven's body, then switch back to your own body and blame the assassination on him. What's the second idea?" I hoped my tone made it clear that blaming it on us was no longer the plan.

Raven cleared his throat. "Why don't we just kill your brother and you can switch our bodies back when it's done? Pay us off and we'll disappear to the Northern Kingdoms or the Islands of the Southern Sea or some other place that is far, far away."

He did have excellent focus; it was the plan that made the most sense, at least for our continued well-being. Although Miaqi's first plan was ruthlessly efficient, repetition should make this second proposal familiar enough that it would seem most logical. If we had time to convince them.

That was the moment when the mage turned to look up at us from the first landing. "It would make sense, sister dear. If I hadn't taken matters into my own hands and forced that foolish mage of yours to make a different switch, it might have worked. Now I have her and soon I'll have the throne as well."

We all stared at him. He'd been so convincing as the mage. Miaqi went very pale. Life had been so much simpler back when we just fought battles for money and stole things. I wanted simple again, any kind of simple. I was also closer to Prince Herali than anyone else. I swung my fist hard at his jaw as the sound of feet on the stairs below us echoed through the stone corridors. I connected and the prince reeled back with an oath. I could see his fingers start to glow again and I lunged forward, Raven at my heels.

I wondered what he was going to do until I realized that Raven's fingers were glowing too. Miaqi was right behind him, Raven's sword in her hand. The prince snarled and yanked a dagger from his robes as I hit him again.

This time, I noticed the ring on the mage's hand and realized that it matched the one Raven was wearing. Raven must have been thinking the same thing and grabbed for it. When his glowing fingertips met the ring's green stone, there was a flash of light. Miaqi touched it an instant later and the three of them lit up like a Festival night fire.

Startled I fell back, tripped and rolled down the stairs to the next landing. I hit the stone wall hard. Which is why I missed seeing exactly what happened next. When I crawled back to the steps and looked up, there was a gray cloud settling like swamp mist above me. Then it disappeared. I couldn't see any of them, but I could hear the prince's men running up the stairs below me, racing to respond to whatever they thought would be waiting for them.

There was no other sound. I scrambled to my feet and ran up the stairs to the landing, trying not to fall over. The walls swam around me. Raven, Princess Miaqi and the prince all lay still on the stone floor when I got there. For a moment, I thought they were dead. I checked my cousin first.

Or at least what I thought was my cousin. I placed one hand on her breast and leaned down to see if I could feel her heart. The slap that struck my cheek made my head ring even more. Princess Miaqi glared up at me out of her own eyes. "Unhand me." Her snarl was impressive.

I yanked my hand back and stood up. That left two possibilities for where Raven was now. I reached for Raven's body, more cautiously this time. I managed to avoid the flailing arms as he woke up from his magical slumber. Then I grabbed him by the throat to get his attention. "What did you say to me the night we left Tacred, cousin?"

Raven stared at me, wide-eyed. It wasn't his voice that answered. "Here we go again. I said that we shouldn't be forced to marry each other. That we could take our swords and go to the Sunborn court and find glory and riches there." The mage's voice filled the landing, sounding weary and annoyed. "We know how that turned out. Now we have to run, Maeve. They're almost here."

Miaqi grabbed the sword and held it to what used to be Raven's throat. "I think you assassinated my brother," she said, steel in her voice.

I grabbed Raven's new arm and we ran up the stairs to the tower, though not without a backwards glance at his former body. The Prince only screamed once before his armsmen arrived. We kept running, knowing what would happen next.

Princess Miaqi would convince them that she had avenged her brother's death. She would find her mage, currently occupying the Prince's body, and have her take over someone else's body. Prince Herali would be given a Sunborn's funeral and Princess Miaqi would be Queen Miaqi. It was ruthlessly efficient.

Our part was done. I looked at my cousin's new body and wondered how long it would take to get used to him this way. At least he could pass for a young man if you didn't know what to look for. But now he was nothing at all like my muscular cousin with his scarred face and his dark eyes that made women melt. I missed him as he was, but there was nothing to be done about that now.

We found the hidden door in the tower. Raven turned and smiled at me with his new mouth as I found the catch and the door opened. It was a very disturbing smile. It made me think of towers and horse piss and people who thought nothing of taking over your body for their own purposes. Not like Raven at all, or at least not like he used to be.

He held out his hand and I looked down at the ring. It still had a pale green glow. "Do you like that body, Maeve? I'm thinking we could make some changes."

My guts twisted. What if he didn't take "no" for an answer? I was done with changes. I wondered if Roderick could help me get into the King's Guard. Boring guard work would be just the thing. I could use my wages to buy an inn. Or do just about else except this.

I backed away from this stranger who might or might not be my cousin. I truly didn't know who he was anymore. I wondered if this was Raven or the mage or maybe Prince Herali. How many people could occupy the same body without leaving something of themselves behind? I didn't really want to know. In that moment I knew exactly what I didn't want: to change into someone else. "I like this body just fine, Raven."

We looked at each other for a long moment, and something in his face shifted. He seemed like he might be Raven again. Or at least a version of him, though transformed in more ways than one. His face glowed with enthusiasm and purpose.

"I think I know how to do it, cousin. When the rings touched out there, I finally understood it, understood how to use my magic," He looked down at his hands, so very different than the ones he had only the day before. "No more futile campaigns or endless battles. I can really be a wizard now."

I almost smiled at the wonder in his voice. He might be power-mad and dangerous, but underneath it all, he was still my cousin, Raven. More or less.

"What will you do if I leave?" He was clearly hoping that I wouldn't object.

And I didn't intend to. "Buy an inn or maybe turn Guard. Something dull and predictable." We smiled at each other.

Then he laughed and shrugged. He walked to the tower window. "I'll miss you, cousin. I'll come back and visit. But for now, I have a lot to learn."

He stared outside for a long moment until his whole body began to glow around the edges, then just as suddenly he was gone. I dashed over to see a raven nearly tumble out of the sky before it righted itself and began flying unsteadily away from the tower.

I watched him go, then looked around for more gold, taking all that I could find. Enough, perhaps, to buy the Rat and charm a clever woman who might warm my bed and order me around. When I listened at the secret door, the stairs below were silent. I slipped down them and out of the palace, bound for a familiar inn and a second chance.

Catherine Lundoff is a transplanted Brooklynite who now lives in scenic Minnesota with her wife, bookbinder and conservator Jana Pullman, and their cats, the latter of whom are ostensibly Egyptian in origin. In former lives, she was an archaeologist and a bookstore owner, though not at the same time. These days, she does arcane things with computer software at large companies and hangs out at science fiction cons in her spare time.

She is the two-time Goldie Award-winning author of *Night's Kiss* (Lethe Press, 2009) and *Crave: Tales of Lust, Love and Longing* (Lethe Press, 2007) as well as *A Day at the Inn, A Night at the Palace and Other Stories* (Lethe Press, 2011). She is the editor of *Haunted Hearths and Sapphic Shades: Lesbian Ghost Stories* (Lethe Press, 2008), winner of a 2010 Gaylactic Spectrum Award Best Other Work. She is also the co-editor, with JoSelle Vanderhooft, of *Hellebore and Rue: Tales of Queer Women and Magic* (Drollerie Press/ Lethe Press 2011). She periodically teaches writing classes at The Loft Literary Center in Minneapolis and elsewhere. Her website is catherinelundoff.com

CPSIA information can be obtained at www.ICGtesting.com
Printed in the USA
BVOW021907051111

275353BV00001B/3/P